This book is a work of ~~fiction~~. ~~The names~~, characters, places, and incidents are products of the writer's imagination or have been used fictitiously and are not to be construed as real. Any resemblance to persons, living or dead, actual events, locale or organizations is entirely coincidental.

She knows too much. Including dark secrets about her sexy protector.

Jennings Abel is undercover for the FBI Task Force known as Sentry. His mission? Take down a biker gang with a drug ring spanning several states. Just as he's getting close, he makes a huge misstep. Defending a woman was *never* in the plan. Neither is roping her into keeping his position under wraps.

Wren is willing to do whatever it takes for her kid brother, but when she's kidnapped by a drug dealer thanks to his screw-up, how far is too far? Soon she's dragged into an even darker game by an FBI agent posing as a biker. She isn't sure if Jennings is using her or hell-bent on protecting her from the gang with his questions about what happened to their top drug dealer. The only bright spot is that if she has to be saddled with a protector, at least he's sexy *and* great in bed.

When it comes to his beautiful fake girlfriend, Jennings is *definitely* off his stride. Keeping her safe—and satisfied—is starting to outweigh his drive to end this dirty operation, and Wren can't help but fall for the alpha bad boy. As this deadly game escalates, Wren and Jennings refuse to fail...but the biggest threat might actually be to their hearts.

JUSTICE FOR THE COWBOY

BY

Em Petrova

Chapter One

Jennings Abel should have a whiskey in his hand. He should be sitting alone at a dinky bar in East Canon, Colorado, eyeing up the pretty bartender who poured his drinks.

He should be watching her full breasts bounce with every move she made. Half the men in town went there to see her on Friday and Saturday nights.

Ah, yes. Jennings could use a little eye candy while knocking back shots.

Instead, he was sitting at a bar the next town over, being served drinks by a tattooed ex-con named Dean while babysitting a bunch of criminals. *But* he'd reached a new inner circle. That made it all worth the suffering.

Just being invited to the Shadowlands bar gave Jennings a position in the biker gang he'd spent months infiltrating.

He brought the whiskey to his lips. The glass was greasy either from sitting on some shelf or never being washed at all. His bet was on the latter.

He slammed the shot and then set the glass down with a *thunk*.

Two of the guys he'd come here with gave him twin head bobs of appreciation. What first impressed the Disciples about Jennings was his ability to hold his liquor—something he showed them on a regular basis. He was the only guy in the club who could drink that much and still remain completely lucid.

"Get my brother another!" Karl called to Dean. The bartender didn't pause to glance at Jennings to gauge if he'd had enough. He just poured the shot and slid it across the bar to him.

Jennings grunted in thanks and wrapped his fingers around the glass.

Being here brought him one step closer to the *inner* inner ring. The final layer of this crooked operation would then be peeled back. Soon he would take down the entire operation.

Jennings and the FBI task force he worked with, known as Sentry, had spent nearly a year getting to this stage. Since Jennings had the best chance of fitting in with the biker gang, he started by hanging around them. Then, once he was invited to the clubhouse, he made himself useful by offering to buy beer or perform other errands.

Soon he was being asked to tag along with them on various "runs" that usually involved a secretive exchange in a dark alley or parking lot and ended up back at the clubhouse draped in whores and smelling like booze.

A feminine hand curled around his chest and nails raked down to his abs. The smell of cheap perfume and cheaper tequila hit Jennings's nostrils. He settled a hand over the one inching toward his dick and twisted his head to meet the stare of the blonde draping herself over him.

"Hey, sugar. You one of the Disciples?"

He stretched his shoulders, angling to the side to show her the leather cut he was wearing and showing off the official patch. He'd been patched into the club not ten days before.

"They don't make guys like you anymore." She leaned closer, bringing the scent of sour breath laced with tequila. She nuzzled his neck. "Why don't you take me for a ride on your hot bike?"

He brought the shot to his lips. Knocked it back. The alcohol burned a path to his stomach. "I think you've had too much to drink. You couldn't even stay on my bike." He looked over her head at the group of women giggling and waving at him. "Your friends want you."

With a small nudge on her ass, he sent her back to the group.

"Another," he grated out to the bartender.

Karl and his other companion Mack stared at him hard enough that he felt their gazes drilling into him.

"What?" He leveled a look at both.

"You gay, man?" Karl's already stiff countenance was even less animated than usual.

"Yeah, we never see you with any women." Mack was nicknamed after the semi-truck for his size. Being

3

six-six and two hundred fifty pounds made him the biggest man in any room.

Jennings huffed out a laugh. "I'm not gay. I just don't go for women like that. I like to leave the best STDs for all of you assholes."

For a second, neither of them got the joke. Then they burst into loud laughter that turned a lot of heads their way.

Jennings's lips quirked at one corner and he chuckled even as he realized his slip. He needed to fit in with these guys, even if it meant drinking to the point of a daily hangover. While he wasn't willing to go to the clinic for gonorrhea, he needed to make it look like he stuck his dick in some pussy.

He set his boot on the floor and pushed off the barstool. "Gotta piss."

As he walked away, he made sure to exaggerate his walk and make it look like he'd had a bit too much to drink. Some major partying in his early twenties gave him a high tolerance for alcohol, but he needed the guys in the club to let down their guard with him. He needed into that final circle—the one that picked up the drugs from over the border.

He needed to see how the church pastor was involved.

After checking to see that no one was around, he placed a call to his boss. Clay Lexis demanded regular check-ins, and Jennings was going to get his ass chewed for going a few days without calling.

"It's me," he said as soon as Lexis's voice filtered into his ear.

"About damn time, Abel. We had an agreement."

"I know. But I'm closer."

Silence hung between them for a moment. "How close?" Lexis asked.

"I'm patched in. We're hanging at the bar."

"Good. Keep—"

Glass smashed and the crash of splintering wood hit his ears. He quickly stepped into the bar in time to see his cohorts kicking a couple other guys' asses.

Karl gripped a man around the throat while another dude whipped out a knife. Jennings started forward to keep his fellow Disciple from being stabbed, but three other guys distracted the assailant by flipping their table.

With the phone still locked to his ear, Jennings edged closer to watch the fight. His "buddies" seemed to be holding their own. Mack grabbed a beer bottle off the nearest table and smashed it over the head of the guy wielding the knife. He dropped like a rock to the bottom of a river.

"What the fuck's going on, Abel?" Lexis demanded.

"Just a bar fight."

Another huge crash sounded, and Dean rushed out from around the bar, baseball bat in hand.

"Sounds like more than a bar fight."

5

The explosion of gunfire stopped Karl from strangling the life out of one of the Disciples' enemies. Jennings's gaze darted around the room, searching for the path of the bullet even as the odor of gunpowder burned his nostrils.

"Jesus, was that a gunshot?" Lexis's voice elevated.

"Just a little scuffle," he assured his boss.

"Scuffle?"

A man raised a chair into the air and brought it down hard over another guy. He collapsed, blood pouring from a gash in his head.

"I'd call it a skirmish," Jennings said.

Another gunshot blasted through the bar. People screamed and stampeded to the exit.

"Jesus Christ, Abel. Get the hell out of there. I'm not calling your momma in Tennessee and telling her that she lost a son."

"She's got four more," he said dryly, watching the progression of the brawl. The Disciples seemed to be holding their own. He didn't need to jump in quite yet. They wouldn't appreciate it if he did—it would make them look weak.

"How's the construction coming on Livingston's house?" Jennings turned the subject.

Lexis grunted but went along with the subject change. "He's making the basement into the Sentry office. There's an outside entrance so it will be easy to come and go."

"Great. Can't wait to see it." More loud thuds, followed by another bullet whizzing across the now mostly empty bar.

"If you live long enough to."

"All good here."

"Stay safe, Abel. I know you always feel like you have something to prove, being the youngest man on the team."

"Nothing to prove. I'm good."

"You're not good. You take too many risks."

In the background, he caught his brother, Julius's, voice. "I should be in there undercover, not Jennings."

Irritation rippled through Jennings. His asshole brothers had somehow convinced the rest of the Sentry team that Jennings was incapable.

"Just because I'm the little brother doesn't mean I don't know what I'm doing."

He ended the call and jumped into the fray.

* * * * *

As soon as Wren got home, she wanted two things: a shower and her bed. Ever since that patient at the nursing home had gotten sick all over herself, Wren craved hot water and plenty of soap. Anything to get the scent of it out of her head.

She'd benefit from heat on her sore muscles too. Being an LPN meant she got the worst jobs in the establishment. One of the tasks she performed most was lifting patients and moving them around to keep them from getting bedsores.

She pulled into the parking lot of her apartment building and cut the engine. With a sigh, she looked up at her apartment door — and froze.

All the air wheezed out of her lungs at the sight of a man standing in her open doorway. She never handed out keys to her place. Nobody knew where she hid it either. The only person who would know that...

"Danny!" The name exploded from her with a mix of concern and joy. She jumped out of the car, grabbed her purse by the long strap and ran for the door.

If nothing was wrong, he wouldn't be here. But the closer she got to her brother, the more she realized it was worse than she first thought.

At ten paces away, she caught his stare while closing the gap between them. When she reached him, her nostrils pinched at the horrid reek coming off him.

Any other person would throw a drug addict right out of their house, brother or not. Especially when he broke in.

But she pressed a hand to Danny's chest and shoved him inside. She slammed the door shut behind them and dropped her purse on the floor.

"What the hell are you doing in my apartment?"

"I didn't have anywhere to go." His eyes darted left and right. His hair was unwashed and hung in lank tendrils around his face. It looked like he hadn't bathed in a week or more. That accounted for the smell.

"Sis. You gotta help me. The guy fell. He *fell*."

Her chest tightened more than it usually did when Danny came around. Usually he only asked for money.

"Who fell? And how? Did he trip?" She had training. She could help.

He shook his head hard. "My buddy pulled a knife. It was so dark, but I saw the blade. He...fell!"

Wren pushed out a sigh. She should have thrown her kid brother out of the apartment when she had the chance.

"You're high, Danny. What are you on this time?"

"I'm not on *anything*. Not today, anyway. The guy fell, Wren. I'm tellin' you, he murdered him!"

Her medical training kicked in again. If Danny didn't use any substances today, it was possible he was experiencing hallucinations from withdrawal. He most likely had come to her hoping she'd give him money for his next fix.

"Look, Danny—"

"The drug dealer killed someone in front of me!"

His earnest tone got her attention. She searched his eyes and saw for once they were clear.

"Tell me what happened, Danny."

He raked both hands over his head. "He told me, 'This can be you next!'"

Wren fought to keep it together. Her brother had a way of dragging her into his world, where she did not belong.

As usual his presence brought drama to her life. Despite all she'd done to help Danny get clean, he always ended up back out there on the street. It broke her heart and frustrated her to the point where she had to force herself to stop thinking about it or go crazy.

He often showed up babbling. Usually nothing he said made sense until he asked for money. This had to be one of those times.

Then she dropped her gaze to his thin body...and saw it.

Blood splatter.

She grabbed him by the arms. "Danny, tell me what happened again!"

"The drug dealer killed a guy. Right in front of me!"

Ice filled her veins. What her brother was mixed up in was no joke. People died from his lifestyle all the time, and a lot of violence had been reported around the city lately.

"He told me that I could be next, Wren. You gotta help me!"

She had to do something. Hadn't she made a silent promise to their late parents to always look after her younger brother? Some days were harder than others—Danny never made it easy on her—but he was the last of her family.

She steered him toward her bathroom. "Get in the shower. Clean up. I'll lay out some clothes on my bed. Put those on when you're done."

He gave a wild nod. "All right. I'll do that."

"We're going to talk, Danny."

"Sure, Wren. Anything you say."

Anything she said? That would mean checking himself in to a treatment facility.

She guided him into the bathroom and waited for a minute outside the door. When she heard the shower running, she rushed to her purse to find her phone.

In minutes she had a drug addiction rehab located and called the hotline. These places came with mediocre success rates and hefty price tags, but what choice did she have? She would find the money. She'd sell something.

Though her low-paying job left her with little money to spare, and she didn't have much either.

She glanced around her apartment at the shabby, thrifted furniture she kept as nice as possible. Her car, then. She could sell her car. It might not be worth much, but it would be a start.

11

When Danny emerged from the bathroom wearing sweatpants and their father's old University of Colorado T-shirt, her heart gave a hard squeeze. God, Danny looked so much like their dad.

"Better?" she asked.

He nodded and sank into the kitchen chair. When he bowed his head, her heart lurched. Danny wasn't himself. Well, he wasn't the person he'd become since drugs started controlling his life.

He really witnessed a murder and been standing close enough to be splattered with blood.

"I found a rehab for you."

His head jerked up. All the other times she suggested that he enter a treatment center, he fought with her and took off again, gone for months.

But this time…he nodded. "I'll go."

Her heart froze in her chest at the look of terror in his eyes. "You're serious."

He bobbed his head. "I gotta get out of town before he kills me too."

"Danny, did you tell this person you were coming here tonight? Does he know where I live?"

"No. I'd never put you in danger, Wren."

Maybe not on purpose, yet he had. He could have been followed. The sooner she got him to that center, the better.

Her frayed nerves seemed to unravel even more. Or maybe they wound tighter. She never could figure out her feelings when it came to...well, most of her life.

"You're skinny, Wren."

Danny's statement had her snapping to attention.

"I don't have much time to eat."

Or the will to eat. Most days she was so sick and scared that her last living family member was out on the streets or worried about making ends meet on her crappy paychecks that her stomach hurt too much to put food into it.

She went to the fridge and got out the leftover cold pizza, from two days before. She set it on the table in front of him. "You can eat this in the car on the way to the center."

He nodded and reached for the food.

The night was a blur of emotions and exhaustion. The hour-long drive to the facility seemed to take forever, and during that time Danny kept trying to give her details about the murder he'd witnessed.

She stopped him each time, but she could fill in the gaps far too easily for her peace of mind. She checked him in, giving her credit card information in hopes that she had enough of a credit limit to keep him there for a few days until she figured out something else.

Then she drove home, feeling emptier than she ever had in her life.

By the time she stepped into the much-needed hot shower, her nerves were far beyond frazzled. She let the water rush over her skin and filled her palm with a copious squirt of bodywash. She just felt icky—inside and out.

If only she could scrub her brain, but her mind never slowed down as it flew over a plan. If she got out of the shower now, and it took her the usual fifteen minutes to fall asleep...she'd still get five hours of sleep before tomorrow's shift.

But the hot water felt *so good* after her long day. Maybe she could function on four and a half hours of sleep.

Expelling a frustrated sigh, Wren switched off the water and wrapped herself in a towel. Maybe she should try to eat something. Nibble on toast.

When she stepped into her bedroom, a cry burst from her throat.

A man was sitting on her bed. Waiting for her.

Fisting the towel tighter, she backed up a step. "Who the hell are you!"

"Where's your brother?"

Panic swept her. She should have *known* that Danny was followed here. This had to be the drug dealer.

All the sick dread swirling in her stomach after finding her brother in her apartment and hearing his story, plus the midnight run to the rehab center, had eased during her shower. Now it crash-landed in her gut like shards of glass. She took a step back but stumbled over nothing.

14

The drug dealer stood, extending to his full, menacing height, towering over her. "I'll ask you one more time. Where. Is. Danny?"

She shook her head. "Not here."

"But he came here. You saw him."

She shook her head with more force. "I don't talk to my brother. He's always in trouble, and I'm trying to lead a decent life."

His gaze shot to the nurse's scrubs she'd stripped off next to her bed. "I can make you talk, woman. Tell me where he is!"

Fear numbed her brain and made her fingers tingle. She probably wasn't breathing, which was lowering the oxygen levels in her system. After a few more minutes, she'd pass out.

She couldn't pass out.

"Danny owes me money." His gaze raked over her, up and down, up and down, lingering on the thighs that the towel didn't cover enough of and her breasts bulging from the edge of the cloth.

The drug dealer gave a slow nod as if he'd made up his mind about something. "He owes me money...but I'll settle for you."

She let out a gasp. "Settle for me?"

"Yup. I could use a good woman. Get dressed. You're coming with me."

"I am not going anywhere with you!"

He gave her a look that said she wasn't very bright. "Of course you are, sweetheart."

"Don't call me sweetheart!"

"Oh, you're feisty too. Even better. Okay, I'll figure out what to call you later. Meet me in the living room in two minutes." He started toward the door.

"I can't leave with you!"

He swung back, piercing her in a heavy stare. "You can and you will," he said slowly. "If you want to ever see your brother again. By the way, you call me Viper."

With that, he sauntered out of the room as if he hadn't just ordered her to leave with him—or said that he'd settle for her.

Settle for her doing what?

A dozen possibilities flew through her tired brain, none of them good.

She hurried to grab some clothes. What choice did she have? She had to get Danny out of this bad situation. Now that he was in rehab, he really had a chance. She would *not* blow this for him. Also, if she didn't go, she'd just end up dead in a ditch.

But was she really attaching herself to a man called Viper?

Chapter Two

Karl leaned hard on Jennings as he limped across the threshold of the motorcycle club. The guy was bruised and bleeding, but the grin he wore told everybody that he had no regrets about the fight.

As they entered the main room, several Disciples leaped up from the couches they were lounging on. "What the hell happened?" The vice prez, Cole, shook a half-naked woman off him. As she stood, her top slipped down to her waist to reveal a perky breast.

"Had some fun down at Shadowlands." Jennings assisted Karl to one of the chairs.

As soon as he plopped heavily into it, several club girls came running to fuss over him. While they wrapped around him, a particular brunette moved in toward Jennings. She always tried to work her charms on him. He didn't welcome her attention.

She lifted a hand toward the cut on his brow. He dodged her but softened the move with a smile.

"Take care of him first." He twitched his head at Karl. The man required stitches, but would probably settle for a butterfly bandage and live with another scar. He also had a nasty bullet graze on the back of one thigh. He was damn lucky the .44 bullet wasn't lodged in the muscle — or worse, an artery.

With an exaggerated pout, the brunette moved away, and Jennings sauntered up to Cole to fill him in on the fight.

"Some assholes down at Shadowlands picked a fight with the wrong guy."

Cole snorted. The man might reek of vodka and the pussy that every woman in the club was all too eager to give him, but Jennings knew he was stone-cold sober and as serious as a stroke.

"You guys teach them a lesson?" Cole asked.

He grinned. "One they won't forget." While Jennings hadn't started any of it, he *had* finished it. Just like his momma taught him back in elementary school when a bully picked on him. While that little prick on the school bus taunted him, Jennings held off all four of his big brothers, claiming he'd handle it.

Once they got off the bus, he hung back, knowing the bully would too. He still remembered his brothers all glancing at him over their shoulders, prepared to jump in. He waved them off.

The kid threw a punch, but he never even got in a full swing before Jennings knocked him out cold with one jab.

Cole eyed him up. "Let one of the girls clean up that cut on your brow."

"I got it." He started toward the bathroom where one of many first-aid kits scattered throughout the clubhouse was stashed.

"Jay."

He swung back at the name he'd given the gang.

"You're going on a run."

"Tonight?" His heart kicked up a notch.

"Tonight."

He answered Cole with a hard nod. "I just need a minute."

When he shut himself in the bathroom, he considered taking out his phone and shooting Lexis a text, but he couldn't risk getting a reply from his boss at any point after this, not if he was on a run.

After he cleaned the wound he'd taken from a broken beer bottle and made sure it was free of glass shards, he stepped out into the main room. Cole stood talking to the tall, greasy-looking guy they all called Bones for his skeletal appearance.

They both looked up at Jennings.

He made his way across the room, circling the pool table and a game that would go on long into the morning hours and continued by the couch where a guy was getting a blow job. Jennings didn't need to glance down to know he already had several shades of lipstick wreathing his dick from the club girls.

He shouldered his way around a few more guys talking to Mack about the bar fight. When he stepped

19

up to the vice prez and Bones, he nodded to each. "What's up for tonight?"

"You and Bones are heading out. Bones knows what to do. He'll show you."

Again, he nodded. "Got it."

Cole gave him a solemn look. "I count on that."

He might be undercover, but Jennings still felt the weight of that statement. Cole was putting trust in him—something that wasn't easily earned. An unbidden feeling of pride swelled in his chest. Being chosen to contribute to a crime wasn't something to be proud of, but he'd spent months working toward this.

Bones turned to him. "Ready?"

"Lead the way."

They left behind the smoke-filled club, boots crunching on the gravel in the parking lot. They bypassed the row of Harleys lined up along the wall, and Bones climbed into a black van.

Jennings took shotgun. During the ride, he knew better than to ask where they were headed. He had to be prepared for anything from raids to violence between the Disciples and a rival gang.

As they drove out of town, his mind moved in a dozen directions. He always had a loose plan in the event that shit went sideways, and this could get deep.

The town of Spring Valley wasn't large and soon the houses thinned. He knew this route all too well since he'd been traveling it for months now.

They were heading to the outskirts of East Canon where the Sentry headquarters was situated.

A dark thrill hit his stomach even as a realization dropped over him like a sheet.

This was it. He was even closer to the end game than he'd told Lexis.

They were going to the church.

The building looked normal enough. A sign out front invited the public to all services. On the outside, everything was on the up-and-up.

But Sentry and the FBI had been on to the happenings for a while now. It started with Lexis's wife getting in deep enough to witness some dirty activity there. Then the pastor went off the grid.

Bones's lighter flared as he lit another cigarette. Smoke filled the van. He held out the pack to Jennings.

"Thanks, man. I'm good for now."

"I never see you smoke."

"You know I prefer the good stuff."

"Oh yeah. Cigar smoker." He bobbed his head.

"That's right." He didn't actually enjoy smoking much at all—he only did it for show. He might be one of the Disciples, but he did all of it on his own terms.

Bones parked behind the church. The few lights out front gleamed in the darkness, and Bones cut the headlights before they turned into the parking lot.

"This is it. Just do what I tell you." Bones jumped out of the van.

"Got it." Jennings followed.

As soon as they were inside, the scent of candlewax and old paper flooded Jennings's senses. The place was silent as the grave. Bones led the way down a corridor and into one of the rooms. He snapped on a light.

Jennings glanced around.

The space was filled with boxes and crates. Plastic totes were stacked along a wall. What they contained was anybody's guess, but he and Sentry believed that drugs were being moved through this very church and that the man masquerading as a pastor was behind it all.

Bones waved at the crates. "We've got to move all this."

Jennings walked around the boxes, already scoping out a spot to plant a voice-activated recording device. Tucking one under the baseboard molding seemed like a good option, as did concealing it in the slats of the window blind.

He looked to Bones for direction. "Where do we move it to?"

He walked to a door across the room. When he swung it open, Jennings's breath came faster.

Two coffins were lined up side by side. Sentry knew drugs were being transported by way of coffins and a couple hearses, two things the authorities didn't look closely at.

"We move the boxes into that room with the coffins?" Jennings acted dumb.

"No — dump the contents of the boxes *into* the coffins."

Before he could respond, a guy with lank brown hair and a pinched face like a weasel walked in, ignored Jennings and settled his stare on Bones.

"You good to go, man?" The weasel looked as antsy as an addict.

"I gotta take a piss. Jay, you get started." Bones tilted his head toward the boxes.

Weasel walked back out and Jennings trailed behind. As soon as he stepped into the space, he spotted trouble.

A woman huddled in the corner as far away from the coffins as possible. She was thin — too thin. He'd seen enough club girls who abused drugs to know when that was the issue, but he'd say that wasn't the case here.

Her hair was too shiny. While pale, her skin radiated health.

He looked her over closer. Her hair was deep brown, like the toasted pecan pies his gramma used to bake for holidays. The locks were damp, the ends drying and fluffier than the rest.

When she lifted her gaze to his—and immediately slid it away—he noted the dark bruises under each.

Fuck. He knew the look of fear and exhaustion all too well.

Weasel shoved open the lid of a coffin and dumped the contents of one box into it. Baggies of cocaine slid against the satin lining.

Jennings ripped open the flaps of his box and followed suit. Out of the corner of his eye, he saw the woman's hands clench into fists.

She looked shaken. Who wouldn't be, witnessing such a thing?

The weasel turned his head to look at her. She thrust her chin high and squared her shoulders.

Jennings and Weasel went back and forth between rooms, filling the coffins with drugs.

Bones came out of the bathroom and began stacking crates close to the doorway so Jennings could grab them quicker. At one point, both Weasel and Bones were in the other room, leaving Jennings alone with the woman.

He couldn't let her see what he was about to do, but he moved to the window and flipped open a slat to peer out at the blackness outside. The recording device that was no larger than one of the pimples on Weasel's face slid off Jennings's finger and adhered to the vinyl.

The woman said nothing about him peeking outside but continued to shoot him worried glances.

He hated seeing any woman in a state of mind like this. It happened at the club all the time, but those women chose that life. This one didn't seem to be in the same league as them.

He longed to put her at ease, but what was there to say?

When both coffins were filled to the point of overflowing, Weasel shut both lids and latched them. "Gimme a hand." He set his hands on top of the coffin.

Jennings did the same, and they pushed it toward yet another door. Weasel opened it to reveal the dark parking lot and a waiting hearse. The engine was running and the back was open like a black yawning mouth, ready to receive the coffin.

*****

Wren's eyes wanted to slide shut. Fatigue crashed over her like an ocean wave striking a cliff. Inside, she was shaking with fear even as she felt numb to the world.

Viper had dragged her on several stops and left her locked in the car before forcing her into the church. The heavy silence and the dim lighting didn't help her fatigue. At this point, she'd been awake about twenty hours and even curling up in the corner next to the coffins sounded good about now.

Could this day get any longer? She'd listened to her kid brother babble about a murder. She'd driven him to rehab. Now she was watching men from the renowned biker gang, the Disciples, load drugs into — of all things — a coffin.

She didn't care what she saw at this point. All she wanted was sleep.

You wanted to be a doctor. Doctors stay awake for long stretches of time.

After the guys pushed the coffins out the door, she was left all alone in the room.

This was her chance.

She ran to one door and found it locked. Then she ran to the other and jiggled the locked handle, a cry of frustration boiling in her throat.

She looked around frantically. There was no other way out.

Might as well join them.

With no other options, she sank to a metal chair and waited for whatever came next.

The silence worked under her skin. Her eyes slipped shut but opened again immediately.

Her head dropped and she caught herself drifting off.

She got up to pace, unwilling to let her guard drop.

The door opened, and Viper walked in.

She scrambled to her feet. "Why am I here?" she demanded.

"You already know too much."

"That's on you. You brought me here. But yes, I know too much about what my brother claims to have seen," she bit off.

Viper's small eyes slit even more. "Stop asking questions."

"I want to leave." She gave him her haughtiest look.

The corners of his lips twitched.

Oh, god. His amusement over her attempt to gain some grip on control was *just* as frightening as seeing that blood all over her brother.

"Why's that, sweet thing? Are you in a rush to get back to my place?" Viper dropped his gaze to her breasts.

A shiver ran through her. Just the idea of being forced into sleeping with this vile man was a knife to the stomach.

"Witnesses disappear, you know." His smile widened.

At that moment—thankfully—the door opened. The big, muscled, scary-looking biker who'd helped load drugs into the coffins entered.

He jerked a thumb at the opening behind him. "He needs you. Says there's a call." His tone was ice cold and gave nothing away.

Viper shot her a look before walking out of the room.

That left her alone.

With the big, scary guy. Not only was he big, he resembled one of those guys who got into a fighting ring and mopped up. His muscles had muscles, and his jaw was so angular that he probably sharpened his knives on it.

Big knives.

She *couldn't* show how much he intimidated her...but exhaustion was winning out. Her brain was so disconnected from her body. She felt like she was swaying on her feet and any minute she'd fall over.

A loud voice penetrated the wall as the phone was put on speaker in the other room. Wren jumped and whipped around to stare, trying not to wince at every word that dropped.

"There's no money! Where is the goddamn money?"

The person stammering out an answer had to be Viper, but she couldn't make out what he was saying.

"There's no money, Viper! And no goddamn body!"

"I have the sister for collateral."

The blood in her veins turned to ice.

"She's a nurse at the home. She'll get me pharmaceutical-grade drugs. I'll sell those. You'll get your money."

Her gaze snapped to the biker standing a few feet away from her. Was he keeping her from leaving? How fast could she make a break for that door or open a window to jump out?

Panic crawled through her insides like a dark, gluttonous beast.

"You're a nurse."

Her head jerked toward the guy.

"Can you look at something for me?"

Oh for fuck's sake. People did this to her all the time. The minute someone learned what she did for a living, they started plaguing her with their ailments. She'd heard it all, from arthritis in their joints to a cough that never went away. One time she'd diagnosed a woman on the bus with a thyroid tumor based on the bulge in her throat. But instead of flat-out sharing her suspicions, she recommended that she see a doctor for the bump.

But *this* was too much. After all that happened today, she was already hanging by a thread.

She gritted out a noise. "I don't even want to be here. Leave me alone."

His dark gaze moved over her face. They weren't exactly kind eyes, but they weren't evil either.

That didn't mean anything. She knew what the Disciples did.

"I got this tattoo," he went on.

She stopped short of rolling her eyes. Probably a heart with a dagger like the rest of the gang.

Wren shoved out a sigh. "Dirty needle?"

He shrugged.

29

Staring at his chest with black cotton stretched across it and a leather vest sporting the Disciples patch worn over it, she questioned why she cared whether or not this man had a festering wound from a bad tattoo. He probably killed people and deserved to die a painful death.

He continued to stare at her.

After a long minute, she caved.

With a resigned shake of her head, she waved her fingers. "Let me see."

He stepped forward. As he grabbed the collar of his T-shirt and tugged it down to expose his pec, she held her breath.

The hard, rounded muscle was totally blank, the skin unmarked by a tattoo or any sign of a wound.

She sucked in a breath.

In that heartbeat, she realized what he was *really* showing her—he wasn't with the gang.

Their gazes met.

In the other room, the voice on the phone grew to a roar as the speaker reamed out Viper and the other guy. Then the call abruptly cut off.

The door flew open and slammed off the inner wall. Wren jumped, and the biker—who wasn't a biker at all—stepped away from her.

Viper strode across the room, bearing down on her. She didn't even have time to blink before he wrapped his fist around her hair and dragged her forward.

30

A shrill scream burst out of her. Pain tore through her scalp as he yanked the strands out by the roots.

"Come on!" Viper barked in a hard voice.

With his stronghold on her hair, she had no choice but to rush along in his wake.

"Let her go." The harsh grit in the big guy's voice sounded with an edge of warning.

Viper stopped dragging her and whipped to face him. "You're new here, but you'll learn. This is how we treat bitches."

He took a step closer, nose to nose with Viper. "*This* is how we treat assholes."

He didn't get a chance to cock his fist before Viper pulled a knife.

A big arm sent her flying backward, but not before she realized that Viper was out-classed in size, strength and skill. The biker lunged for Viper. Their bodies arced through the air, landing hard on the floor.

The biker rolled to his feet, and so did the jerk keeping her captive. A scream built in her throat. She staggered farther away, pitching up against the wall. Pain radiated through her shoulder and down her arm.

She never tore her gaze from the fight. Viper leaped forward, knife extended. The lethal point swiped inches away from the biker's toned midsection.

The biker dropped into a lower stance and danced around him. "Let's go, motherfucker. Show me what you got."

Viper darted forward again, knife outstretched.

It happened so fast that she almost missed it. The biker grabbed Viper by the arm and bent it around.

Next thing she knew, the handle protruded from Viper's gut.

The biker released him, and Viper hit the floor with a sickening thud.

Wren stopped breathing.

She glanced between her protector and the man on the floor.

Her tormentor was stabbed. Bleeding out.

No, he was already dead. Judging by the position of that blade, no medics or surgeons could save him.

Her gaze flew to the biker's.

He stared back at her. "Well, this complicates things."

Chapter Three

The Harley's engine growled, the headlights cutting through the dark streets. The cool wind ruffled Jennings's hair.

His momma would give him the sharp edge of her tongue if she knew he was riding without a helmet. Or maybe she'd be glad she raised him to be a gentleman who gave up his own helmet for the woman seated on the back of his bike.

Hell, he didn't even know her name. But the feel of her pressed against him, her arms circling his waist, was now burned into his psyche. Every turn they made, every mile they rode, he learned more about the woman.

She didn't need to speak for him to know that she was broken—and fighting it. The fire in her eyes contrasted the dark rings of fatigue beneath them. The proud tilt of her chin told her that while an asshole might try to drag her away by her hair, she wouldn't have put up with it for more than a few steps.

But she didn't need to worry about how to break free anymore.

Jennings had handled matters for her.

Now they had a body to deal with. Lexis would be pissed. His brother Julius would give him hell for it.

What went down next probably scared the woman gripping him hard around the turns most of all. Jennings told her to sit down and wait for him. Then he returned to Bones and told him that Viper bugged out.

"Good. I don't fully trust that asshole." Bones twitched his head at Jennings, and they went out to the hearses they'd loaded the coffins into. With each behind the wheel, they drove to a cemetery. Rather than the small-town church cemetery where parishioners went to their resting places, they went to a big one in the next town.

Bones told him it kept the cops off their asses, and after what he saw next, he understood why the cops hadn't caught on to their scheme.

They delivered the goods to a mausoleum. In a hearse. At night. Several trucks were parked in the lot, all of them with logos for a landscaping service. Each truck hauled lawnmowers and tools for keeping the cemetery looking neat. In the winter, they would have snowblowers.

When he walked by one parked truck, he glanced in the bed. Big tool chests would be the perfect spot to transfer the drugs. Most of the vehicles were empty, but he recognized a guy from the club. Even dressed as a groundskeeper, he stuck out as one of the Disciples.

34

Sure enough, they unloaded the contents of the coffins into the mausoleum drawers. He guessed that the goods were then transported to various spots in the area via those trucks.

After that, he told Bones to drop him at the club so he could grab his bike. Then he took the route back to the church — and the woman waiting for him — at high speed.

With her safe for the moment, Jennings took a detour on a longer route through the city just to check something out. If his hunch was right, he'd see at least one of those trucks parked at the Shadowlands bar.

Sure enough, a landscaping truck was parked in the lot. And he'd lay down his hefty savings that the driver didn't stop off for a beer.

When they took the last turn that led to the building temporarily serving as Sentry headquarters, the woman tightened her hold on him. The urge to cover her arm with his hand and soothe her worries away swelled in his chest. He didn't act on it.

A minute later, he rolled into the parking lot. Gravel crunched under the tires. After he parked, he twisted his head to speak to his rider. "You can get off."

She hesitated for a minute. Then very slowly swung her leg over the bike. After he dismounted too, he held out his hand. "I'll take the helmet."

35

Wordlessly, she unfastened the strap and removed the headgear. She held it out to him, and he hung it on the handlebar for the next ride.

There weren't any security lights out here, and that meant he had to look harder at her in order to see what she was thinking or feeling about being in an unknown place with a complete stranger.

"I don't even know your name," he said quietly.

"It's Wren."

He nodded. "I'm Jennings. Come inside. And let me do the talking."

"I have no intention of speaking to anyone in there."

The wind sent some litter tumbling across the parking lot. He punched in a code and opened the door. Golden light spilled out, cast over the woman's face.

Wren.

He waved a hand for her to enter first. She did, and he silently closed the door behind them. "Straight to the end of the hall. Door on your right."

She stopped dead. "Where are you taking me?"

"I promise I'll explain more once we're inside. You don't need to be afraid."

"That's exactly what someone who intends to harm me would say!"

Her sassy comeback caught him off guard.

"Am I being sex-trafficked?"

His brows pinched. "Hell no."

"Is this a whorehouse?"

"Jesus. Not at all. Come on. They're waiting for me." He didn't wait for her to follow him. Truth was, she could turn around and run right back out that door and no one would stop her. Of course, *she* didn't know that.

Her footsteps sounded quietly behind him.

As soon as he entered the room stacked with computer equipment and surveillance screens, three people spun in their chairs to look at him. Julius, Livingston and Lark had all been manning the system.

Jennings was about to fuck up their night.

"The prodigal son has returned." His brother Julius's dry drawl prompted a huff of a laugh from Livingston.

"Took ya long enough, Abel." Quaide Livingston looked past him and fixed his stare on Wren.

No point in sugar-coating things. "I fucked up."

Julius slowly pushed to his feet. Livingston did the opposite and leaned back in his chair. Lark just clucked her tongue like a sad mother hen whose chicks didn't cooperate.

"Who do you have with you?" Livingston asked.

"This is a witness."

Julius eyed Wren as though she were strapped with explosives. "Witness to what exactly?"

"We were at the church. We got back from the run—don't worry, I'll fill you all in—and some asshole started abusing her."

Lark popped to her feet, and Livingston straightened in his seat.

Wren banded her arms across her chest in a protective pose. On the surface, she appeared collected, but all of them could plainly see that her hair wasn't bobbing around her shoulders from the air currents in the room. She was trembling.

Again, that strong urge to touch her and put her at ease rolled through him.

"Get Lexis in here. He needs to hear this," Jennings said to Lark.

She issued a low sigh. "I'm warning you. He's already been awake for thirty hours. You know how he gets all hopped up on energy drinks." She walked out of the room to fetch their team leader and her significant other. When Lark passed Wren, Jennings noted how Wren dropped her gaze to Lark's midsection and the very obvious baby she carried front and center on her small frame.

He captured Wren's attention. "Can I get you something to drink?"

"Um…no."

He took that as her needing a drink but refusing in case they'd laced it with some drug that would knock her out.

A second later, heavy steps thudded in the hall. Lexis entered, eyes bloodshot and hair mussed like he'd been roused from his sleep.

"Abel," he said in a gritty voice. "Lark said you fucked up."

"I killed a guy."

The air was sucked out of the room. Beside him, Wren turned to an unmoving statue.

Lexis cut a hand through his hair. "Start talkin'."

"The guy she was with had her by the hair and was dragging her across the room. I intervened, and he pulled a knife. There was a small skirmish—"

"You and that damn word," Lexis growled.

He plowed on, "Short story is that I directed the knife back at him, and now he's dead."

"Jee-zus, brother," Julius bit out.

Lexis leveled Jennings in his hard glare. "So you dropped a man and took off with his girl?"

"Pretty much."

"Did you do *anything* right?"

"I saved her, didn't I?"

He glanced at Wren. Fear crept into her already shocked expression.

He locked eyes with her. The depths of her baby blues were as dark as a wild sea.

"I'm undercover." He used the low tone reserved for frightened dogs.

Her eyes widened.

"And you're not really that good at it." Julius's comment made Jennings swing his way, middle finger in the air.

He and Julius shared a glower. "Look, I could have done things differently, but now I need backup."

Lexis pushed out a sigh. "Okay, here's what you're gonna do. Go back to the clubhouse. Make everything look good."

Jennings nodded. "We need cleanup for the body while we still have the cover of darkness. There won't be anybody at the church right now. They're out on drug runs."

Wren issued a low moan.

Automatically, he moved to her side. "This is my team." He stabbed a finger at each person. "Lexis, Livingston, and that asshole is my brother Julius."

Before he could get to the last member, Lark spoke up. "I'm Lark."

"I'm Dove." The voice from the doorway had everyone pivoting to see the second pregnant woman coming forward. Right behind her was the third wife of the Sentry team and his brother's own wife.

"I'm Avalynn."

Wren's stare shifted from person to person. After a long heartbeat, she said, "I'm Wren."

"Ahhhh!" Lark's cry had her husband grabbing her arm.

"Are you in labor?" Lexis demanded.

"What? No. I've got months and months left to cook your son here. I'm screaming because…well…she's one of the birds!"

All gazes fell on Jennings. He could practically hear the guys' thoughts—what was he doing with a woman who had a bird name? Lark and Dove were obvious bird names. Avalynn stretched the limits, with the meaning of her name being beautiful bird. But Wren?

Dammit, I am not getting more tied up with this woman.

Lark touched Wren's shoulder. "Stay here with us. It's safer."

Wren gaped at her.

The guys started talking at the same time.

"Get the body cleaners—"

"There's not much time to waste."

"Someone should go in with Jennings."

He whipped his head around and glared at his brother. Being the youngest of five brothers always came with a level of protectiveness that pissed him off. If they weren't protecting him, they were trying to do his job for him. He was far from incompetent, and nobody else could infiltrate the biker gang the way he had—or become one of them in so little time.

"She's going to stay here with us." Lark's announcement broke through the rest of the voices.

Wren tipped her jaw up. "No, I'm not."

The way she made that declaration tugged at a thread in his chest.

Lark shook her head as if she didn't understand. "But you're safe here."

"I can't stay here. I need to keep my brother safe. I have to act like everything's normal or...they'll kill him." Her voice broke as she swung her stare to meet Jennings's. "He witnessed a murder."

A weight dropped into his gut. This woman had things to tell him. Maybe more than the things he had to confess to her.

The gears in his mind ground. "Did anybody see you when you were with Viper?"

She shook her head. "He made a few stops, but he forced me to stay in the car. Then he took me straight to the church."

"Good." So he could take her with him. She needed to go about her routine, and so did he.

They needed each other.

His stare connected with Wren's. "I have to take her."

* * * * *

"You're not going anywhere until we've fed you." Dove swung around and walked back out of the room.

42

Quaide, the guy they called by his last name Livingston, watched her go. "No point in arguing with a pregnant woman about food."

"He's right." Avalynn was right behind Dove with Lark on her heels.

Wren looked to Jennings, waiting for the next move even though the last thing she wanted to do was hang out with these people or eat. Her stomach was knotted and she felt dizzy with exhaustion. All she wanted was her own bed.

His gaze traveled over her face. The urge to duck her head and hide from that probing stare tore through her, but she was made of tougher stuff and let him look his fill. Whatever he saw made him nod.

"We'll stay for a bit. We need to discuss the plan anyway."

He curled his fingers around her elbow. The warmth of those strong yet gentle fingers almost made her knees buckle. Right now, she could lie down on the floor and happily pass out for twelve hours—if she didn't have to be at work in only a few hours.

When he drew her forward in his wake, she had no will left in her to fight. She followed him down the corridor to another room. The space had the look of most office buildings, with a low ceiling and bad lighting. But the galley kitchen was spic and span, and there was a long table for them all to sit.

Jennings led her straight to a chair. The rest of the women bustled between refrigerator and table, setting out fixings for sandwiches while the guys filtered in to crowd around the table, clustering in a group at the end as the women took up the other.

Wren stole a peek at each person. The men were huge, stacked with muscle that pointed to some intense training and possible military backgrounds. She needed answers about what this group actually did—and how they could help her—right after she got some sleep. Her brain couldn't hold on to any information at the moment.

Before she knew it, someone slid a sandwich on a plate in front of her. An unopened bottle of water appeared.

"Get used to this, Wren. We have midnight snacks a lot around here." Lark offered her a smile.

Was it even midnight? It had to be well past that. She shot a glance at the window. It was still black outside. How many more hours of sleep could she get if she laid down right this minute?

"You have what it takes to fit in for sure." Lark's statement brought her back to the conversation.

"Right," Dove agreed, lowering her water from her lips. "A bird name."

Wren glanced to the beautiful brunette seated at the end of the table.

"What about Avalynn?" she asked.

"It means beautiful bird," the woman answered for herself. "She definitely has the right name, but…"

Lark and Dove gave her sharp looks.

Avalynn shrugged. She leaned over the table and whispered, "We're talking about Jennings here."

Wren eyed her. "What about Jennings?"

Everyone carefully avoided shooting glances at the big man dressed in the black leather vest of a Disciple but who wasn't actually part of the gang.

"Well," Lark brushed a lock of red hair off her face, "he has little brother syndrome."

Wren was dead in her seat, but just looking at the god of a man had her insides clenching. His strength and confidence had struck her immediately when he walked into that room back at the church. And the way he took charge, making sure she was safe, was even hotter.

"He's always been fling material."

She could have a fling.

Where did that come from? Her fatigued mind shocked the hell out of her.

She had no clue what little brother syndrome had to do with her fitting in with the women sporting other bird names, but she didn't care at the moment.

"Try to eat a little, Wren," Dove encouraged with a sympathetic smile.

She picked up her sandwich. After a few bites, the food started to revive her from her stupor. At the opposite end of the table, the guys were deep in discussion, their voices pitched low. Jennings glanced over and caught her gaze. Seeing the sandwich in her hand, he dipped his head in a single nod and went back to his conversation.

"I shouldn't be wrapped up in *any* of this," Wren burst out.

The ladies stared at her.

She waved the hand holding the turkey and cheese on white bread. "All I did was come home from work to find that my brother broke into my apartment. Next thing I know, I'm driving him to rehab. Finally, after all these years! *Then* I get out of the shower to find this guy in my house. He tells me that he'll settle for me as payment. Who *does* that?"

Her outburst had all three ladies shaking their heads.

"I was going to be a doctor. Now I'm an LPN at the nursing home. It's a good job, don't get me wrong. But it's terrible hours and hard work. I don't mind hard work, but I only did it for the money. I had to help my brother after our parents died."

Lark let out a gasp. "Your parents died?"

She nodded. "My brother got into drugs and I had to either ignore that and continue with med school or take this position as an LPN. It's better than trying to make a living running errands for people on Quick Bunny."

46

"Hey, Quick Bunny isn't so bad." Lark rubbed her pregnant belly.

"Until you deliver a bomb." The sardonic voice from the end of the table brought Wren's outburst of oversharing to a halt.

She swallowed. *Everyone* was staring at her.

An electric current seemed to hover in the air between Lexis and Lark.

"At least her bomb didn't explode." Dove's statement had Quaide's brows pinching into a thunderous expression. "What a way to lose a vehicle," she continued.

"But you gained me..." The man's voice was gruff, almost tender.

"And for it, *you* lost a house."

"Totally worth it."

Wren's attention bounced back and forth between all four of them, trying to understand, to focus on what they were saying and the meaning behind bringing it up. But she couldn't.

She turned to Avalynn. "Why do you look familiar?"

The woman pushed out a heavy sigh. "Tell me you haven't seen all of me."

She blinked at her in confusion.

"Please don't let it be the sex tape."

Wren bit off a chunk of her sandwich. "Forget I asked."

47

"Wren, we've come up with some details about our plan that you need to know." Jennings twisted in his seat to look at her. Even with several feet between them, she felt a strong pull to the man, like he held a cord that was pinned to her.

Lexis cleared his throat, gaining her attention. "Jennings is taking you back. You'll be allowed to go on with your life."

Allowed to? What was he saying?

Jennings's dark gaze penetrated her. "You'll be playing a role, Wren, same as me. While we figure out what went down with your brother, we lie low."

She set down the remainder of her sandwich, her stomach in knots again.

"One stipulation. You can't call and check on your brother in the rehab." Jennings didn't sound even a little bit sorry to drop this bombshell on her.

"Why not?"

"The Disciples could check your phone any time."

"I don't want anything to do with that gang."

"I know, but now you're waist-deep in it. You need protection that I can give you. And I could use your help too. If you play the part of my girlfriend, you're in the club. The women always talk. You report everything to me."

Her heartbeat tripled. Act like his girlfriend?

"I promise I'll protect you and get you out of this mess as soon as possible. But you have to trust me and do as I tell you. Got it?"

Her stomach churned. The food felt like a lead ball in the pit of her stomach. Did she have a choice? Yes. But she wanted Danny to be safe more.

"Fine."

Lark settled a hand on Wren's arm. "Obviously you know Jennings is undercover. He's really good. He'll protect you."

She jerked her head up to look at Lark in surprise. "He already has."

"And you have to protect him too, by following his direction. Outing him to the club he's been infiltrating for months is dangerous to him," Lexis added.

She straightened her spine. "I don't know what to do to protect Jennings, but I'll do anything to save my brother."

The long look Jennings sent her felt like a tender caress. "You already have saved your brother." He pushed his chair away from the table with a low scuffing noise of the legs on the tile floor. "Now let's get you some sleep."

In a few steps, he reached her and helped her to her feet. She felt as if she was swaying but knew from years of studying the human body that she was simply suffering from sleep deprivation.

Without another word, he led her out of the kitchen. When he opened a door and she saw the bed, she nearly collapsed with relief.

In a burst of energy, she made it to the bed and crawled in. She curled up on her side, head cradled by a pillow as soft as a cloud. Her eyes slipped shut immediately but she opened them again when Jennings pulled the covers over her.

She breathed a sigh of contentment.

"Get some sleep, honey." Bracing a hand on the bed beside her, he leaned in, hovering close enough that the clean scent of man and leather permeated her sleepy haze.

He leaned in closer. And closer.

Her heart thundered. Was he going to —

When he dipped his head and pressed his lips to her forehead, emotion broke over her. The tender brush of his mouth was gone as quick as it came. Her eyes slammed shut as exhaustion took hold. But something else had a grip on her — the man who'd saved her from Viper's abuse.

Jennings had killed for her. And the best way to repay him was to do as Lexis said and protect his true identity from the Disciples.

Chapter Four

Jennings ran a knuckle over his jaw, creating a rasping noise against the growth of beard. How did everything get so screwed up?

He dropped forward in the kitchen chair, elbows planted on his knees, and lowered his head into his hands.

Damn. Things had gone sideways in the blink of an eye. Just hours ago he was about to bring down a multimillion-dollar drug empire and the organized crime ring behind it. He'd been invested in this op for a year. He ate, slept and breathed the Disciples. He gave up his own personal life to sink so deep undercover that some days he didn't know who the hell he was anymore.

Now he stood to lose it all. From a single mistake.

He raked his fingers over his scalp. He couldn't believe he'd fucked up this bad. Killing a man in self-defense was one thing. But he couldn't give that as his only excuse.

He was protecting Wren.

When that motherfucker grabbed her by the hair and started dragging her out of the room, the look of pain tearing across her beautiful features enraged Jennings. Every fiber of muscle in his body had locked, at the ready to defend the woman he didn't even know.

After a long conversation with his team, Jennings had a new plan in place. The wild card? It heavily involved Wren.

Earlier at the kitchen table, Lexis had let bits and pieces slip to Wren, but the sleeping woman didn't know the half of it. When she woke up, Jennings would have that talk.

He pushed off his knees and glanced at the time on his phone. She'd only been sleeping for an hour, but he couldn't wait any longer. The Disciples would still be in party mode, most of them far gone from alcohol. It was the perfect time to show up at the club with Wren and flaunt her, to show everyone that she was with him.

The silence in the Sentry headquarters was a constant scream in his ears. His teammates had gone home for the night, and unlike the house they used as the former HQ, this rented space didn't have all the comforting creaks of old walls and floorboards.

As he moved through the empty spaces to the room where his new fake girlfriend slumbered, he couldn't help but dread the task of waking her.

The woman was exhausted. She clearly wasn't eating well either. Stress kept her going, but it was killing her too.

He quietly twisted the doorknob and pushed the door inward. The room was dark, but he made out the small form of Wren asleep on the bed. One arm was flung to the side, and her nut-brown hair tumbled over her cheek.

Jennings stopped. What had made him kiss her?

The feel of her skin beneath his lips haunted him. Never in his life had he felt an urge like that—or as strong either. Yet when he tucked her into bed and pulled the covers over her, the need to soothe her overwhelmed him and he kissed her forehead.

The most chaste of kisses. So why did it make his gut grip so damn hard?

He stepped into the room. In sleep, she made no sound, but he detected the slow rise and fall of her chest.

Waking her felt like a crime. Earlier in the kitchen, she clearly hadn't understood everything that was said. Lexis telling her that she had to play a role to keep the op on track and Jennings from being outed never registered in her brain, going by the confusion in her pretty blue eyes.

He pushed out a sigh and stood next to the bed, staring down at her. Another full minute ticked by. He really should wake her now.

But he stood there for another minute and then another. Watching her sleep felt like an invasion of her privacy, yet in those few minutes he learned so much about Wren.

The tension in her pretty face was diminished by rest but still not absent. She was hanging by a thread, that much was evident. He'd overheard what she told the ladies about their parents being dead and her feelings of responsibility to her brother.

He also heard the way her voice cracked slightly when she talked about leaving med school to work at the nursing home.

This woman was beaten down by life...and goddammit, he wanted to fix things for her.

Everything.

That wasn't in his job description and was well above his pay grade. Nowhere in his contract did it say that he should protect this woman too.

But dammit, he wasn't walking away from her now.

Reaching out, he touched Wren's shoulder.

She jolted awake, sitting up at the very same instant her eyes popped open, wide and round with alarm.

She saw him and scrubbed her hands over her face.

"I'm sorry to startle you, honey."

"It's all right. I was dreaming."

He didn't need to ask what she was dreaming about. The tight set of her lips told him enough.

She darted a look at the window with the closed blinds. "What time is it?"

"You slept an hour. I wanted to let you sleep longer, but we need to discuss some things before we get on the road."

She scraped her fingers through her disheveled hair. Her effort to smooth the strands only made her look more appealingly mussed. Any man who saw this woman would be crawling into bed with her.

Jennings's body wanted that too, but he wasn't just any guy. He had control.

Sinking to the foot of the bed, he made sure not to touch her. "We need to talk about what's next."

She stared at him. "I don't want involved in any of this. I just want to live my life. I want to go to my crappy job and come home, do chores and maybe read a little bit before I collapse into bed each night."

"Honey, you know that's not living, right?"

She arched a brow. "I don't need you to tell me that. But it's what I've got right now. Until I figure out something else."

"That's fair. But you *are* tangled up in it. You put your brother in rehab, and while that is noble and necessary, he is a witness to a murder."

"And you killed the murderer!"

Without hesitation, he nodded, owning it. "I don't like it, but it was me or him. I don't have regrets. But you heard that guy on the phone in the church too—he asked about the money and he asked about the body. I'm not sure where this murder went down, but there's almost always camera footage. I guarantee that these guys will be looking at it and will see your brother there."

"He's still not safe even in rehab, is he?"

"I'm going to do my best to keep him safe there. I've got connections. In the meantime, I need to ensure you're safe as well."

"You plan on doing that how?"

"You're with me. At all times."

She shook her head. "I need to work."

He contemplated her. She didn't exactly look down and out, but her clothes were worn and since she didn't earn a ton of money at her job, money was most likely an issue. Especially since she'd probably just spent a fortune putting her brother into rehab.

"We'll figure out how to keep you working. Meanwhile, I have to return to the club. I'll ask again—the Disciples never saw you with Viper, did they?"

She shuddered. He clamped his fingers into a fist to resist the need to touch her. To settle her. "No. We stopped a few places. I don't know where exactly. Everything was too confusing and he made me stay in the car anyway. Then we went straight to the church and nobody saw me. Unless there was a camera there?"

"I'll take care of that too. It's only been a few hours. It's unlikely anybody's looked at the footage."

"What do we do now?" Her sweet, full lips twisted and she set her top teeth into her plump bottom lip to keep it from trembling.

His gut clenched. He *didn't* want her afraid. He *did* want her mouth.

"We're going to the club. The guys aren't going to ask questions. They'll just know you're with me and therefore, protected. All you do is play the part and act like my bitch."

The long look she gave him brought a chuckle to his lips.

"I see you don't like the term, but it's common in the clubhouse. All I ask is that you stick close to me and if I tell you to do something, know that it's to keep you safe."

"Fine. When do we go?"

"Now."

She muttered something under her breath about an hour of sleep and whether or not she could sleep on a motorcycle. He gave her a moment alone to use the restroom and then led her out to the parking lot.

The deep black of night felt heavy around them as he mounted the cold steel and she climbed on behind him.

He twisted his head to look at her. "Got the helmet strapped on?"

"Yes."

"Good. Now hang on to me."

The rough growl of the engine in the silent streets of East Canon echoed off the rundown and abandoned buildings on their way out of town. The ride might be short, but having a beautiful woman plastered against his back with her arms around his waist tested that control he was so damn proud of.

He had women, but he didn't flaunt them around the club, and he sure as shit didn't take those club women to bed. So walking in with Wren was going to make people take notice.

When he pulled into the club parking lot, she didn't immediately let go of him.

"I don't know what to do in there," she said.

"You don't speak. They'll all be drunk or high and probably won't take notice of you. But just in case, your name is Wendy in there. I'm Jay. Got it?"

"Yes." She loosened her hold on him enough that he could swing his leg over the machine. He helped her off too and with her tucked into his side, they entered the club.

The reek of smoke and sex lingered in the air. He felt Wren stiffen against him.

"Hey, it's Jay! Where ya been, man?"

He gave a chin lift of acknowledgement to one of the guys. "Been having my own kind of party." He drew Wren a little closer.

The dude chortled with laughter although it wasn't that funny. Jennings shot him a sly grin and towed Wren through the room, making sure every person there knew she was with him — and off-limits.

A cloud of smoke in the corner and the stench of marijuana had him leaving a wide berth, but he did parade her by the guys just to make sure they all knew she was his property too.

At the bar on the other side of the room, he stopped for a shot.

"You want one, baby?" he asked her.

Big blue eyes met his. "You said I've had enough, Jay."

The small emphasis on his name wasn't lost on him. She might be acting the part, but she most definitely wasn't going to let him forget it.

The crash of something glass hitting the floor sparked a round of raucous laughter. Wren pressed closer to him, and he drew her more protectively against his side. Someone started up some music with a driving beat and everyone tipped back more booze.

The girl doling out drinks at the bar passed him a shot glass, but he plucked the whole bottle out of her hand and swaggered around the room with it and Wren. Occasionally, he brought the bottle to his lips and pretended to swig. He could hold his liquor but right now it wasn't necessary to do more than put on a good show.

After they'd circled the room again, he dropped into a leather armchair and pulled Wren into his lap. She perched stiffly on him for a moment.

Pressing his lips to her ear, he whispered, "Try to relax."

She turned her head and buried her lips against his neck. The soft, plush feel of her lips sent a sharp pang of need to his groin. The weight of her in his lap and her round ass on his thighs weren't helping matters at all.

"I'm either exhausted or getting high from the smoke in here," she said against his neck.

He cupped her face and nuzzled her as a way to reply. God, she smelled good. Like pears. Fresh pears. "I know you're dead on your feet. Give this another couple minutes and we'll duck out."

She nodded, mouth trailing over his skin. He narrowly swallowed a growl of need and probably threaded his fingers into her hair with too much strength. She didn't complain about him tugging the strands, though.

A couple guys wandered over to talk. Both were clearly tanked on alcohol. But the way their gazes skated over Wren made him edgy. He'd seen a few guys battle it out over club whores. The last thing he needed was someone who'd been a Disciple longer than him challenging him for her.

He couldn't guarantee he'd be able to stop himself—he'd do anything in his power to keep her out of the hands of these men.

60

As he talked to the guys, Wren looped her arm around his shoulders and began kissing his neck and jaw.

His cock stiffened even as admiration for her commitment to playing the role blurred the lines between what was real and what was fake.

"We're going on a run later this week, man. You in on it?" one of the guys asked.

He planted his hand on the curve of Wren's ass and gave it a caress. Her lips stilled and then clamped on his neck in a soft, sucking pull.

Goddamn. He was going to lose it with this woman. Either she had a lot of practice as an actor or...

He could be cocky, but he wasn't going to delude himself that she wanted him that way. She was just putting on a show.

"If the boss man tells me to go on that run, I'm with you." He struggled to keep his tone even. Dark desire clawed at his insides.

"I can see you're busy, man. We'll talk later." He waggled his brows at Jennings before wandering off again.

Wren lifted her lips from his neck.

Their stares locked. Her chest heaved almost imperceptibly.

Goddamn. He was in so much trouble with this woman.

* * * * *

"C'mon." Jennings twitched his head for Wren to follow him. Where was anyone's guess. She hoped it was a bed...for so many reasons.

She placed her hand in his big one, mind swirling with sleep-deprivation and desire. She felt almost drunk with it.

She was far too aware of the man leading her out of the main room of the clubhouse and down a corridor. He drew her into a dark room and flipped on a light. A gold glow washed over his big, muscled body.

He stared back at her, eyes dark. "Jesus, honey. You can't look at me like that."

"Like what?"

"You don't owe me anything."

"No, I don't. Maybe you owe me."

His lips quirked up at one corner, giving him an even more bad-boy look. Her insides fluttered with desire that started the instant he settled her on his hard thighs. When she began kissing his neck, it was only half for show. The rest had been her.

He lifted one hand and cupped her cheek. "What do you think I owe you?"

Darting her tongue across her lips, she held his stare. "You look good to me."

Something moved in the depths of those dark eyes. His jaw firmed as if he clenched it. "I'm glad to hear that, but you don't want to get tangled up with me. Not that way."

She covered the back of his hand with her own. "What if I want you to break my dry spell?"

His nostrils flared. "How long's it been for you?"

"Six months." Even as she said it, she recalled the horrible disappointment of that date. He wouldn't know a clitoris if somebody drew him a diagram. And he was a med student.

Emboldened, she took a step toward Jennings. She placed her hand over the bulge in the front of his jeans, molding her fingers to his thick, hard length.

He groaned. "You're playing with fire, woman."

"You sure it's not the other way around?"

"Fuck. No, I'm not. What the hell are you doing to me?"

"Seducing you." She backed him up a step to the bed. Being the aggressor came with a heady surge of power. Or it could be the aftereffects of breathing in so much pot smoke, or the fact that she had an hour of sleep after being kidnapped out of her apartment and dragged into a dark underworld.

She stroked his cock through his jeans.

A primal groan burst out of him as he locked his hands on her ass and dragged her up against his body. With a grind of his cock into her pussy, he wrapped her hair in his fist and gently tugged her head back.

Her pulse raced. Need spiked. If she was going to be forced to act like his "bitch," the least she could do was gain some pleasure out of it.

"You sure about this, Wren?"

The use of her name brought her down to earth. Her answer remained the same.

"Yes," she murmured.

He leaned in. "You're *sure*?" The scent of man and leather washed through her senses.

Her pussy squeezed. "Positive."

His eyes narrowed. "Give me your mouth."

She tipped her face up to his. When he swooped in and claimed her lips, she let out a small cry. Hooking her arms around his neck, she yanked him down for more. Angling his head, he slanted kiss after kiss over her lips as he rocked his cock against her pussy.

On a whimper of need, she hitched herself up and locked her legs around his waist. Strong fingers kneaded her ass as he took two steps to the bed and collapsed with her.

His chiseled body pinned her down and his kisses drugged her. Passion blazed hot in her core as she realized a man like Jennings might actually *finally* give her the satisfaction she'd been craving all these months. The release from stress that would put a bounce in her step and give her the best night's sleep of her life.

His mouth crashed onto hers. His tongue swept over hers in a slick glide that promised that he was good at using that body part too.

Shivering, she slid her hands under the leather of the vest they called a cut and eased it off his bulky shoulders. He let her remove that and his T-shirt as well.

Once again, when she saw the bare skin on his chest where all the other Disciples sported a tattoo, she stilled. "You're really not one of them."

He searched her eyes. "I'm really not."

"That makes you even hotter." She yanked him back to her, taking control of their kisses for long minutes until she realized he was only humoring her.

He tore from the kiss and went for her neck, latching on with a purpose that told her he was finished playing around. This man knew how to get down to business.

He sucked on her neck. He flicked it with his tongue. He bit into her earlobe and made her pussy flood.

Rocking her hips in wild movements wasn't nearly enough to satisfy this burning need inside her. Only when he ripped off her top and ducked his head to trail his lips over the tops of her breasts did she begin to fathom just how good this would be.

As he bathed the tops of her breasts with his tongue, he unclasped her bra. One tug and she was bared to him.

Lifting his head, he stared down at her breasts. "Christ, woman. So fucking gorgeous."

She cupped his jaw, letting her fingertips trace over the stubble of his beard as he dipped his head to capture one hardened nipple in his teeth.

She cried out.

He tugged.

Her pussy clenched and flooded even more. As he swirled his tongue around the tip of her breast, she lost herself. Small moans filled the room, every one of them coming from her.

When he swiped his callused thumb over her other nipple, she let out a low cry. "Please!"

"Keep on begging, honey. I love hearing it." His teeth flashed white in her line of vision as he bent his mouth to her breasts and worshipped them for dizzying minutes.

She dug her fingers into his shoulders, guiding him, lost in sensation.

Slowly, he trailed his kisses down over her ribs. Reaching the waist of her jeans, he took a minute to scrape his beard over her flesh.

Marking her.

Her pussy contracted, and she couldn't stop herself begging this time. "Your tongue. My pussy!"

"Nothing would stop me."

He tore off her clothes. Spread her thighs.

The look of need blazing in his dark eyes just about sent her over the edge before he ever lowered his tongue to her slick seam and delivered the first lick.

Chapter Five

Jennings's cock was hard enough to hammer steel. His pulse throbbed in time to the ache in his balls.

Burying his tongue in Wren's pussy had him about to lose that grip on control. Her sweet flavor and the throaty cries bursting from her fueled him.

He never left women wanting, but this one... Well, he wanted to give her an experience she'd never forget.

She bucked her hips, pressing her pussy against his tongue. He sank it into her sheath again and again before easing it out and gliding it up to her clit. The hard bud seemed to tremor under his tongue. He gave it a soft flick, and then another.

She raked her nails over his shoulders. If he liked seeing his beard burn on her sensitive stomach, he'd like seeing her claw marks even better.

Doubling his efforts, he sucked on her clit in slow draws of his lips and mouth even as he sank one finger inside her. Her body clenched on the digit. She let out a muffled moan, maybe the sweetest sound he'd ever fucking heard.

Who was he kidding? It *was* the sweetest sound he'd ever fucking heard.

His rigid cock drilled against his fly. The minute he sank into this woman, he would have all of two minutes before his cum was pumping into her. Ever since her ass settled in his lap, he'd wanted this.

Wanted her.

"Yes!" She shuddered. He ground his tongue against her until her release struck with a force that damn near shattered him too.

She came in sharp contractions. He grasped her hips, holding her in place while bathing her pulsating pussy with his tongue and fucking his finger in and out of her.

"Oh god!" She went limp on the mattress, but he wasn't finished loving her.

He added a second finger to her tight sheath, dragging a strangled cry out of her.

He pushed his fingers deep, tunneling, locating her G-spot.

"Ahhh!"

"Come for me again, princess. Come now!" He stroked her inner wall, latched on to her clit with his lips and coaxed a second orgasm out of his lover.

Her juices flooded his fingers and mouth. A growl left him, and he set to work tasting her release with small flicks of his tongue while she writhed for him and even thumped a fist on his shoulder.

When he finally raised his head and pierced her in his stare, he got so much more satisfaction from the moment. Her beautiful face glowed. Her eyes were lit with electric pleasure.

In methodical movements, he stripped off his clothes, then located a condom from a stash in the drawer of the nightstand placed there for any of the guys to use. Most of them didn't bother, but he wasn't that asshole.

Wren watched his every move. When he had the condom rolled over his hard length, she parted her legs and held out her arms. "Come to me!"

He wanted her in all positions. But knowing how tired she was, he would do all the work tonight. Next time? She'd be riding him. It was only a matter of time before she was seated atop him, thrashing and taking his cock the way they both wanted.

* * * * *

Jennings was big. Hard. He stretched her inner walls until she soaked him with more juices.

The dry spell was no more. With this man, there was no such thing as dry.

He held her stare for a long heartbeat as he sank into her inch by inch. Her core tensed. Quaked.

He'd made her have two back-to-back orgasms, something no man had ever done. Hell, she'd never even fucked herself with a toy to that type of screaming ecstasy.

70

As the tip of his cock breached her innermost point, he froze. Her body adjusted to fit him, and he slipped a fraction deeper.

They shared a groan.

"Jennings!" she gasped.

"Gawd, princess. You're. So. Damn. Tight."

He rocked his hips, drawing his erection through her heated walls. Their mouths fused in a hot, tongue-dueling kiss as he began to fuck her. Each slow stroke made her pant. Every hard jerk of his hips made her cry out.

She rarely came from penetration, but Jennings was going to guaran-damn-tee that did not apply to him. Every bump of his mushroomed head inside her pussy sent her rocketing higher.

All of a sudden, she thought of his cum filling her. Never had she wanted such a thing before, and she shouldn't want it now from a virtual stranger. But the mere idea of hot spurts bathing her inner walls sent her into overdrive.

She bucked her hips to meet his thrusts. The tension harnessed in his muscles told her that he was on the edge too.

Their bodies slapped together. She bit into his lower lip.

He issued a primal growl. When he stilled, she held her breath...and felt him let go.

The instant his orgasm struck, hers did too.

Her mind spun end over end. Her pussy contracted hard and fast around his length. Every jerk of their bodies and each flip of their tongues stole her sanity.

The rough pant of his breath mingled with hers as they slowed.

After long minutes, she caught her breath. His lips trailed over her breast, and he delivered a final lick to her nipple.

Sinking her fingers into his soft hair, she closed her eyes on the sensation of finally having gotten what she needed.

"Good, princess?" he rumbled.

"Mmm."

He pulled his cock out of her and slipped down her body. When his tongue hit her sensitive folds—again—she cried out.

Never in her life had a man gone down on her after sex. Each twist of his tongue gathered the juices of her release. When he lifted his head, his lips glistened with her pleasure.

Was it terrible of her to think about calling off work so she could stay in bed with this man? How much more pleasure could he give her if they devoted a whole day to it?

No. She had to go to work. How she'd survive the shift on no sleep was another story, but she needed the money. Especially now that she was paying for Danny's rehab on top of all her own bills.

Jennings climbed off the bed. She watched his hard ass as he walked into the bathroom.

Damn. He was one fine man. She harbored no regrets at all about her impulsive decision to get him into bed.

But now, reality crashed down on her. Her brother had people after him. She was in danger too.

And who knew when this would all end and she could go on living her life, sad thing that it was.

Jennings was right when he said that she wasn't living. She was simply *existing*, and she'd known it for a long time.

He emerged from the bathroom, his chiseled body starting new shivers of need in her, and his dark stare sending her pussy into spasms all over again.

For a few stolen minutes with this man, she'd forgotten all of her problems.

She couldn't wait to do it again.

Chapter Six

Yeah, Wren was thin but those curves he'd had his hands all over were still prominent and alluring as hell.

Out of the corner of his eye, he watched her pull her top over her head. As she stretched her arms up, he glimpsed her ribs. He couldn't count them all, but he didn't like seeing them. Some women were naturally slender, but he could tell from Wren's curves that they once were riper, fuller.

Her stress level was stamped all over her beautiful face and in the slump of her shoulders. He planned on doing something for that, and soon. If he couldn't help her, what good was being in this position?

She tugged the hem of her top down to her waist. "I need to stop by my apartment and get a clean set of scrubs for work."

"It's not safe to go back there until I have backup and check things out to make sure nobody's watching." He slid his cowboy boot on.

She pushed a sigh through her nostrils. "I guess I can borrow a spare set from the nursing home locker room. There are some changes of clothes in case of…" She broke off, her delicate nose wrinkled. "Well, in case."

Not wanting to know more about what duties she must perform in a place where people couldn't take care of themselves, he let the subject drop and picked up another. "I need you to be a hundred percent aware of your surroundings."

She faced him, brown hair waving over the tops of her breasts. "I'm a woman. I'm always aware."

He cocked a brow. "Then how did you get out of the shower to find a drug dealer in your room?"

With a flat look, she slipped on her sneakers. "I'm ready. We need to hurry to get my car."

He shook his head.

"I do *have* a vehicle. It's a piece of shit, but I have one. How am I getting home if you drop me off?"

"No car. I drop you off. That's how this works, Wren."

She opened her mouth to protest, but he moved to stand in front of her. "Let me bring you up to speed. You're not going home. You're staying with me. And I'm gonna take you to work and pick you up."

"What about my clothes and things?"

"Like I said, I need to check out your place first, make sure nobody's lurking around."

"And if they are?"

"Then the Sentry ladies get what you need and leave the bag in a spot where we can collect it."

She pushed out another sigh. He studied the luminous blue eyes that flashed whenever she geared up to argue with him. To his disappointment, she just skirted around him and walked to the door.

"Hold up a second. Let me go out first."

She rolled those beautiful eyes heavenward. "Is the guy who knows my brother witnessed that murder standing out in the hallway now?"

He shrugged, feeling the leather shift on his shoulders. "You never know." With that, he pushed open the door and caught her by the hand as he stepped out. The smell of cigarette smoke, booze and pussy soured his stomach, but it seemed the party was over and he could safely sweep Wren out of the clubhouse without anybody asking questions.

In the parking lot, he handed her the helmet again. "Which home do you work at?"

"The Spring Valley Nursing Facility." When she had it strapped on and was seated on the back of his Harley, he started the engine and rolled onto the road leading to the home where she worked.

During the drive, he swung his gaze left and right, on the lookout for any cars gunning for him on top of his regular awareness as a motorcyclist. Spring Valley was a step up from East Canon where the Sentry headquarters was located. The general filth and poverty with a side helping of despair were absent on this section of road leading to the nursing home.

Small trees lined the sidewalks and they passed a park with a playground. Later in the day, he'd see moms and small kids gathered around the swings and a spiral sliding board. A strip of small trees with rounded tops adorned the median. A few pedestrians lingered outside a coffee shop that had fantastic cinnamon rolls. Sometime maybe he'd take Wren there for one.

The thought of her licking frosting off her plump lips had his cock stretching against his fly.

Waking with her beside him in bed had been amazing. He still couldn't believe he'd slipped and let go like that with her especially while on an op. But the way she'd begged him to lay claim to her sweet body made it impossible for him to walk away.

And if she begged again? He'd give in. Only this time, he was pushing into her from behind just to feel his balls against the tight globes of her ass.

As he passed the cemetery where they'd unloaded drugs into mausoleums, he turned his head, looking for the landscaper trucks. Only one sat at the end of the lot, looking abandoned.

A decoy to throw off the police or anybody else looking too hard. He—and now Sentry—knew better. They were on to the Disciples, and it was only a matter of time before they nailed the bastards down and locked them all behind bars.

When they approached the sprawling brick building of the nursing home, Wren tightened her hold on his middle. He drove into the parking lot and cut the engine.

She climbed off the bike, thigh rubbing against his and sending a sharp pang through his groin again. She passed him the helmet, and he cradled it against his chest.

"What time do you get off?"

"Three."

"Be out front. I'll pick you up at 3:01."

He would have missed the way her jaw set if he hadn't been watching her so closely.

"I'm not staying with you."

"Bless your heart for thinking you can get out of it."

"Bless your heart? I thought people only say that in the South."

He leveled a look at her that lasted several heartbeats.

"I can't believe I slept with a man that says bless your heart," she muttered.

Caught off guard, he laughed. "While you slept, I programmed my number into your phone."

Her jaw dropped. "You—"

Reaching out, he settled a fingertip under the tiny point of her chin and snapped her jaw shut. She jerked her head away.

"You take an awful lot of liberties."

He recaptured her chin between his thumb and forefinger and leaned in even as he drew her a step closer. Her body pressed against his thigh. Her lips parted but this time with what he guessed to be desire, going by her dazed expression.

Good—real good. She looked like a girlfriend would look. He still had game.

He meant to stamp a kiss to her lips but the minute he felt her mouth soften, he groaned and deepened it. Their tongues met in a slick sweep before he withdrew.

"Be here."

That stubborn tilt of her jaw matched the way she shifted her hips to one side. He had to wonder if she was tapping her toes inside her sneaker.

"Look, Wren, I know you're independent as hell. It's apparent."

Happiness glinted in the depths of her eyes. "Really?"

With a huff of a laugh, he nodded. "Really. Now get in there before you're late. If you need me for anything at all, call my number."

She nodded and turned around. Jennings watched every step she took and continued to stare at her until he could no longer see her beyond the glass door.

He had to return to the clubhouse. They'd mentioned another run, but after last night's party, who knew if that would happen.

When he passed the cemetery, he automatically glanced over at the truck...but it was gone.

As soon as he walked into the clubhouse, he spotted several of the guys seated at a table, beers in front of them despite the early hour. Many of them looked to be nursing hangovers from hell. The bloated bags under their bloodshot eyes wouldn't win the gang any beauty awards.

He walked behind the bar and grabbed a beer too. When he sat down with them, he took a deep pull. The woodsy brew hit his tongue, and he swallowed out of reflex and months of flying under their detection.

"What's going on today?" he asked Cole.

The man swung his stare to Jennings's. "Since you're so chipper, you can clean up the place."

He stared back at the man who called almost all the shots that their president didn't deem necessary to bother with himself.

Cole narrowed his eyes at Jennings. "I'm serious, Jay. Clean this dump up."

With an internal sigh, he shoved away from the table, carrying his beer to set on the end of the long wooden bar with a clank hard enough to break glass. Then he went to gather empty bottles, carrying them to the big trash can in the corner.

He tossed them in all at once.

Two Disciples looked up sharply at him, hands protectively cupped to their ears as they nursed their sensitive hangovers.

"Jesus, keep the noise down, would ya?" one muttered.

"Sure." To add more insult, Jennings pursed his lips and began to hum as he continued cleaning up.

* * * * *

Wren carried a wad of dirty bedding to the laundry hamper and dropped it in. The smell of soiled sheets burned her nose, but she didn't acknowledge the intrusion on her senses. How could she when Jennings's words were looping through her head?

He'd listed all the things she couldn't do.

Don't call anyone.

Don't check on your brother.

The man was so damn bossy. He believed he could boss her around just because he saved her from... Well, whatever Viper would have done to her.

She lifted a hand and stroked her fingertips over the spot on her scalp where he'd yanked at the strands of hair. If not for Jennings's interference, who knew where she'd be right now. Viper was capable of violence. He'd killed a man in front of her brother. The way he grabbed her told her that violence extended to women. Add in the fact that Viper's boss had put him in the hot seat, and Wren most likely would have been beaten, but probably worse.

Her stomach was in a constant state of upheaval. The few nausea pills she'd taken from the employee first-aid kit didn't begin to touch the stress she was under today.

She couldn't even leave work due to illness because Jennings demanded that she ride with him. And if she did leave, she wasn't allowed to go to her apartment anyway.

However, the thought of spending more nights with her hot protector *did* appeal. All those muscles just *waiting* for her to look at them, to touch them. His skin was velvet covering steel. His hands perfectly rough, each small callus at the base of each finger exerting mind-spinning sensation on her needy flesh.

And god, the man could lick pussy. The dark pressure of his tongue on her clit—

"There you are."

Jolted from her reverie, Wren focused on the woman standing in the doorway, holding dirty towels.

She flicked her stare from the cheap terrycloth to her coworker and friend's face. "Hi, Janine."

The brunette had been hired around the same time that Wren started working at Spring Valley Nursing Facility, and it provided them an instant bond. They'd suffered together through training and the growing pains of caring for the elderly.

Janine cocked her head to the side, the warm brown eyes that she was known for among the staff and patients scrutinizing Wren. "You look different."

She arched a brow. "Different how?"

"I don't know. Something's definitely different, though."

She extended a hand to the wall dispenser, and antibacterial liquid dispensed into her palm. She rubbed her hands together. "Nope. Nothing's different."

"Oh my god! I know what it is! You had sex!"

Wren gaped at her friend. "How did you know?" she blurted before she could even think about denying it.

Janine bounced up and down. "You *did* have sex! Oh my god, tell me all about it!"

She wrinkled her nose. "Not in here. Let's grab a coffee."

Janine hurried out of the small space and strode to the employee break area. She racked up two paper cups on the counter and sloshed coffee from the pot into both. When she thrust one into Wren's hand, her eyes danced with excitement.

"There. You've got your coffee. Now spill it, girl!"

Wren curled her fingers around the warm drink. The grin spreading across her face was totally unexpected considering the circumstances in which she'd met the man she slept with.

"Well?" Janine looked like a firework about to explode and shoot through the sky.

Wren inhaled the aroma of what passed for coffee around this place. "It was the best sex of my life."

"I knew it by that look on your face!"

How did she look? Her usual expression was pinched with fatigue and her eyes dimmed of any life she formerly had before her life went to hell.

Her insides tingled at the memory of Jennings sinking into her. How his hard biceps flexed with each jerk of his body.

She leaned in to whisper to her friend. "I've never had such amazing sex. Ever!"

Instead of bouncing up and down again, Janine cocked her head to study Wren. "Are you sure it was the best?"

"What do you mean?"

"Maybe you think so because it's been so long."

She took a swig of coffee. "You're right. I should probably do it again to be sure."

Janine giggled and held up her paper cup. Wren bumped hers gently against it so as not to spill either drink and give them something else to clean up around here.

She glanced at one of the hundreds of clocks the nurses relied on for everything. "Damn, I've got to do meds." She took another mouthful of coffee before setting aside the cup. She'd never come back to finish drinking it, and later on, she'd have to toss it in the wastebasket.

She and Janine walked out of the break area and started gathering the medications their patients took on a daily basis.

As she worked, she focused on the task. Messing up and giving the wrong medication to the wrong person could spell disaster. Even though this was far from her dream job, she was conscientious about her work. She came every day. She gave her all to keep people healthy and comfortable.

She was distracted too, and not just from the memories of Jennings's mouth trailing over her breasts to her belly and making his slow path downward between her thighs. She had a hell of a lot to worry about, like pretending to be the girlfriend of a Disciple. Just being seen with a man wearing that patch on his leather cut invited a level of danger that she didn't want anything to do with.

After double-checking on every medication and patient it would be administered to, her mind freed up enough space to consider Janine's question. *Was the sex that good? Or was her friend right and she only thought so because it had been so long?*

The multiple orgasms Jennings gave her said oh hell yeah, it was *that* good.

Her insides knotted at the memory.

As she pushed the cart of supplies from room to room, again checking the patient's ID against the medication received, thoughts of being in Jennings's bed again threatened to intrude. She kept pushing them down over and over until the very last cupful of pills was set before the final patient on her rounds.

"Your stomach medication, Mr. Mario." She put some brightness into her tone and earned a rare smile from the older man suffering from dementia.

He brought the small cup to his lips and tipped the pill into his mouth.

"And your water to wash it down with." She held out a cup with a straw.

After he'd taken a sip and leaned back against his pillows again, Wren pushed her cart out of the room. One of the other nurses intercepted her.

"There's a call from Mr. Mario's family. His sister calling for her weekly check on her brother."

"Oh, sure thing. I'll take the call now."

Wren dropped off the cart and went to the phone behind the nurse's desk. She took a lot of these types of calls from concerned family asking about health updates or even checking to see if a package arrived for their loved one. She had enough med school under her belt to know much more than an ordinary LPN or even an RN. While she had yet to interact with real patients on that level, this job had taught her a ton about relations with patients and their families.

She spent about twenty minutes talking to his sister about Mr. Mario's health and habits. Assuring her that the man wasn't just stuck in bed staring at the four walls of his private room eased her mind, but conveying that he often went to group activities in the home was more of an indicator that his morale was good.

Once the call ended, Wren experienced one of the highs of the job. This stuff made it all worthwhile.

She started down the hall to check on some patients who liked sitting in front of a big picture window overlooking a garden. Birds flitted around the trees and shrubbery, much to everyone's delight.

As she started around a corner, a deep voice caught her attention.

She froze in her tracks. That *voice.*

Icy fear washed over her. Goose bumps rippled up and down her spine and broke out all over her arms.

She knew that voice.

All of a sudden, she was back in the church, and the man who brought her there was speaking to a man on the phone. The man she heard right now was the same guy who'd told off Viper.

Her heart thundered, pounding against her ribs. She could barely catch her breath. A wave of dizziness almost bowled her over, but she grabbed on to the doorframe to hold herself upright.

She had to see who was talking.

Could she peek around the corner?

Her fingertips dug into the frame. She couldn't do it. She was too scared.

Her spine steeled. No—she was strong. She'd buried her parents and guided her brother through a lot, including finding him a place in rehab. Those things were far from small.

She darted her head out and stole a peek at the hallway. In a single glance, she took in every detail of the man talking to one of their housekeeping staff.

She ducked behind the doorframe again, imprinting the man's appearance in her brain.

Tall. Slender. Sporting a trim mustache. Dark brown hair. His forehead sloped back to a receding hairline, and his clothes were nice.

Too nice for around here. He looked like he just came from Los Angeles or New York City. Wren didn't have much in the way of her own wardrobe, but she knew good quality clothing when she saw it.

His shoes and belt were high-end leather. His trousers were cut to fit his slender build to perfection. Even the polo shirt he wore seemed tailored for him.

Only a man who made a lot of money dressed like that. And no wonder, considering the number of bags being loaded into those coffins. He must earn a fortune selling illegal drugs.

She had to tell Jennings.

The man ended the conversation. For a long minute, she strained to hear more from him. When she heard nothing, she poked her head out again to see him all the way at the end of the hallway, walking at a leisurely pace toward the exit.

Before she could call Jennings, Janine called for her help on an emergency that cropped up. By the time she clocked out, a strong case of the jitters hit. She quickly changed back into her street clothes, grabbed her purse and practically dashed out of the building to find Jennings waiting for her on his bike.

Their gazes locked. Concern flashed over his rugged features, but she didn't take time to respond to that look. She ran up to his bike, stumbled and almost dropped her purse. But she managed to reach the bike and throw her leg over it.

Latching her arms around his middle, she said, "Get someplace where we can talk!"

"Hang on, princess." He hit the gas and they sped away from the nursing home that had become more than a place where she labored day in and day out for low pay.

Now even her workplace wasn't safe.

Chapter Seven

Jennings climbed off his bike. The urgency in Wren felt like a punch to his senses, and he wasn't going to waste a second finding out what was behind it.

He unfastened the helmet she wore and planted his hands on her waist, holding her in place.

"What happened?"

Her eyes darted left and right. "Can we talk somewhere else?"

"We can talk right here." They were outside the club, but no one was around. The cameras the Disciples used for security were low quality and mostly for show to keep thugs from trying to steal parts off their bikes in the lot.

"Are you sure? I don't feel comfortable here."

"Talk to me." The grit in his voice was unintentional but her stare flew to his and held for an endless heartbeat.

"Someone came to the nursing home today."

"Who?"

"The guy who was on the phone with Viper. You know, in the church."

He didn't give any indication of what was going on in his mind—he just stared at her for another long moment. "You're sure?"

"Totally." A shudder tore through her.

"Okay. I'll look into it. Just try to relax."

"Relax? Here? Are you nuts?"

The door opened on the building on the far end of the parking lot from them, but he couldn't risk any suspicion. He ducked his head and trapped Wren's sweet lips under his.

She let out a low humming noise that sent spikes of need to his groin even as she melted into his touch.

God, the woman was so responsive. He didn't think it was just an act either, and damn, that pumped up his libido.

He let his fingertips graze her side. She issued another sound.

In a swift move, he yanked her off her feet and pinned her to the building. Her eyes flared wide with surprise before he settled one hand over her breast, thumb swiping the point of her hardened nipple.

"Jennings!"

"Shh, baby. You're so keyed up. Let me calm you down."

"Here? In the open?"

He glanced over his shoulder. The guy who'd exited the clubhouse was climbing onto his bike. He dipped his mouth to the column of Wren's throat.

She smelled amazing. So feminine. Her natural pheromones had him by the balls and damn if he could shake off this want. One night was *not* enough.

He'd only meant to kiss her for show. Now the Disciple was rolling out of the parking lot and there was no need to continue the act.

As he teased the tip of his tongue over the soft portion of her neck below her dainty earlobe, his cock hardened to full mast. Only one taste and he wanted more.

She set her fingers into his shoulders. "J—"

"Jay," he filled in for her before she slipped with his real name again.

She stilled. "Jay."

He raised his head and pierced her in his stare. "We need to go inside. Are you up for this?"

She shook her head. "I don't know."

"I believe in you."

Her brow creased in the cutest of skeptical looks. "You would be the only one, then."

Her comment startled a bark of laughter from him. He leaned in and stamped a soft kiss to her full mouth before straightening to his full height.

"Just follow my lead."

"I'll do what I can."

As he caught her by the hand and led her across the gravel to the entrance of the club, he thought about that statement. Coming from a woman with the kind of fortitude she displayed, he guessed that her lowest effort far surpassed what others gave of their *all*.

When they walked in, several guys called out greetings to him. Jennings gave them chin lifts of greeting but kept his arm securely around Wren. A few of the women who hung around the club shot Wren dirty looks.

"Why are they looking at me like that?" she whispered to him.

He leaned in to kiss the top of her head. "I've rejected all of them at least three times."

Approaching the bar, he slowed his steps. Cole twisted on his stool. His stare hit Wren and lingered for a beat too long. She mashed herself closer to Jennings, and he held her firmly.

Cole shifted his attention back to him. "I'd like to talk to you a minute."

"Sure, what's up?"

He looked at Wren. Seeing that the vice president wanted her to make herself scarce, Jennings reluctantly released her. He gave her a small pat on the ass, sending her across the room to the table of ladies that already disliked her because she'd earned a higher position just by being on his arm.

A Disciple wouldn't give attention to his woman over his VP, but it took a lot for Jennings to keep from turning his head to watch her walk away.

"Pour our man a drink, Hound," Cole said to the guy behind the bar. The new recruit was swiped directly from Shadowlands.

The guy set a glass on the bar and poured him a double. When Jennings fisted the vodka, he stole a sideways glance at Wren. She stood with the ladies and seemed to be holding her own. A couple of them had stopped shooting glares at her.

"Got a job for you, Jay."

He twitched his head to eye his VP. "You know I'm here for anything." Even as he said it, he knew he could be getting in deeper than he ever had. He hoped that was the case.

"Slam that drink and follow me."

Jennings tossed back the alcohol and shoved away from the bar. "Let's go."

Cole climbed off the stool, straightened to his full height and shouldered his way through the group to the back room.

Jennings had been in here only once before. The space was stacked with crates of alcohol. Today a folding table was set up in the center and two guys stood at it with open boxes in front of them. As he looked on, one man withdrew a bulky parcel from the box and placed it into an open duffel bag.

Cole waved toward them. "We need another packer."

"I'm your guy."

"Good. Show him what to do." Cole walked out, leaving him to it.

Jennings took his place at the end of the line. The man next to him nudged a box his way. "Packs of ten in each bag."

"You got it." He'd handled more drugs on this op than any before this, and he was glad to have enough experience at it to keep his expression bland. He wasn't shocked by much anymore, least of all drugs being loaded from crates into bags.

"Who gets the bags?" he asked in an offhanded manner.

One of the guys shrugged. "We pass them out to dealers. They choose where to distribute."

"Got it."

"When you pack Viper's, don't forget he gets twenty instead of ten." The statement from the other man made Jennings pause.

Viper wouldn't be distributing any parcels of drugs. Not when Sentry had sent cleaners to collect his body at the church in East Canon.

"Think he'll show his face?" the first man asked.

"Yeah, why not? This is his contribution to the club."

"He hasn't been around in a couple days."

Jennings looked between the guys. "Do you mean the skinny guy? Shorter than me? Has stringy-looking brown hair?"

"Yeah, that's him."

He grunted. "I heard he couldn't handle it. Took off."

"No shit?"

"Seriously, man. I heard it down at Shadowlands." He continued to fill the duffel, making sure the parcels of drugs were tightly packed before zipping it shut.

"Guess we don't need that bag for Viper, then. I'm making the executive decision to give Viper's cut to Freeman." The guy looked at each of them. "What do ya say?"

"Sounds good to me." Jennings shrugged and grabbed another bag off the stack.

Damn, that was the first lie he'd actually told since coming to the club. Rule was that you stuck as close to the truth as possible. Easier to lie that way.

Then again, maybe it wasn't such a far stretch to say that Viper couldn't handle it and took off. Just that he couldn't handle *Jennings* — and he'd taken off in a body bag.

In little time, they finished their task.

"Let's go grab a drink. I could use one. Handling all that heroin makes me jones for something in my system." The guys moved out ahead of Jennings.

He threw one more look at the corner, mentally counting the bags stacked there. Twenty-two by his estimate, and each one had ten parcels. All but the one meant for Freeman, who was now Viper's replacement.

When he stepped into the main room, he sought out Wren. His gaze skimmed several women and landed on her.

She was sitting in the lap of a guy they called Darius Dark.

He had one hand inching up her thigh and the other beneath her shirt.

A red flash of fury exploded in Jennings's mind. At that moment, Wren looked up. Fear written across her face.

In several strides, Jennings reached them. He ripped her out of Darius Dark's lap and shoved her behind him.

Darius Dark's eyes narrowed to slits and his knuckles cracked as he clenched his hands into fists.

Jennings widened his stance, placing himself between Wren and the man who'd been groping her. "Hands off my property," he gritted out in a voice loud enough to boom through the room.

Chatter halted. The club rang with silence.

Darius stood, elongating himself to stand an inch or two above Jennings. No matter. He was more than confident in his ability to fight.

"The woman was enjoying herself," Darius sneered.

"Honey, were you enjoying yourself?" He didn't look at Wren when he asked the question.

"No! He forced me into his lap even though I belong to you, Jay."

He cocked a brow at Darius Dark. "See? You must be deaf. Don't let it happen again."

"Go ahead and make me!"

He cocked his arm back. Wren's fingers wrapped around Jenning's biceps.

All he could see was that terror on her face mingled with disgust and this bastard's filthy hand working under her shirt, kneading her breast like it was a chunk of bread dough.

"My. Property," he bit off.

"Stop! Please." Wren's soft whimper broke the chokehold of fury coursing through him.

He dropped his arm, almost yanking her over with his power. Before she could fall, he swept her against his side. When he felt how much she was shaking, he damn near lost his shit.

He would end that guy.

What was one more death in the club?

Cole positioned himself between Jennings and the man he wanted to dismember. Slowly. Hell, he'd even do it in front of witnesses.

"Let it go, Jay. You know Darius Dark is a pussy hound. He won't touch your woman again."

Jennings held Darius Dark's gaze for a long heartbeat laced with menace. "Make *goddamn* sure you don't."

Cole nudged the man. "Go on home for the night, Dark. Come back tomorrow."

He grunted, his lip curling when he faced Jennings one last time before crossing the room to the exit.

Cole gripped Jennings's shoulder hard, fingers biting into his muscle. "You good now?"

"Fine," he said tonelessly.

"Go have a drink. Let your lady return to her girl-talk with the other women."

Jennings met Wren's gaze. In those stormy blue depths he saw that she didn't really want to speak to them. Maybe she didn't even want to be away from Jennings after what happened. But in the end, she patted his chest and pulled away from his side.

He watched the smooth glide of her hips as she returned to the table of women. Not unsurprisingly after that confrontation, they accepted her into their fold as if she'd always been their friend rather than a newcomer who stole one of the available men in the club.

Assured of her safety from more creepy bikers, Jennings followed Cole to the bar. His muscles were still locked for battle. His chest on fire with anger.

He might be playing a role, but his reaction to that bastard touching Wren was *all* too real.

* * * * *

99

As a rule, Wren didn't drink. But she accepted the cheap wine cooler a woman named Tilly placed in her hand. She brought the sour apple drink to her lips and downed a big swallow.

After having that man's hands all over her, she needed the numbing of alcohol.

She twisted to glance at Jennings. His broad back faced her, the leather straining across the width. The tension in his shoulders was unmistakable even to her, and she didn't know him that well.

My property.

She didn't belong to anybody and would fight tooth and nail for that truth. But in this case — coming from Jennings — the words impacted her in a totally different way.

Almost as if…she *liked* it.

She needed more than alcohol. Hell, a therapist probably couldn't even help her now.

Tilly and some of the other ladies were comparing notes about who'd slept with Darius Dark and how handsy he was with them too. Wren nodded and tried to focus on what they were saying, but hearing that she was just another of the biker's conquests didn't make her feel any better.

"Hey, everyone!" The tall guy roped in muscle bore the vice president patch on his vest, along with a lot more patches that showed how deeply involved in club life he was. "Jay and I are heading to Shadowlands. Who's with us?"

A cheer went up. Wren's mind flinched away from the harsh noise. She glanced at Jennings just as he started toward her.

When his rough, warm hand closed around hers, she clung to the solid strength of the only person in the place she wasn't afraid of.

She tipped her face up to his. "You're leaving?"

"*We're* leaving." He leaned in, lips brushing across hers in the scantest caress. "I'm not leaving you behind. I'm sorry — I can't do it."

The pain in his tone had her lifting a hand to cup his stubbled jaw. What was she doing? She couldn't believe she was trying to offer *him* comfort.

Minutes later, she was on the back of his bike, flying through the city. Purple shadows played over the streets of Spring Valley. Lighter violet shades kissed the sky as night fell. The scenery and the fingers of wind teasing her hair made her question if she was dreaming or all this was real.

It wasn't her life. Last week she was simply working to get by like anyone else. In hours, her entire life flipped upside down, leaving her questioning if she'd made the right choices from the get-go.

If she had let her brother deal with his own problems...if she had continued with medical school...things would be very different.

She wouldn't be wrapped around a man masquerading as a member of the deadliest biker gang in this part of the country.

But he made her feel safe too. Jennings had proved he had the means to protect her.

My property.

Were those lines from the role he was acting out? If so, he was more skilled than she ever guessed, especially since the dark fury flashing in the depths of his eyes was so believable.

The bar was situated on one of the streets she'd never visited before due to the bad reputation, but the inside had a warm, pub feel that put her more at ease. Before Jennings left her with the ladies, he pressed his lips to the side of her throat.

"Be on watch."

Before she could ask what she was watching *for*, he drew away from her and joined the guys at a long table near the bar.

Tilly seemed to enjoy her company and took a seat next to Wren. She was grateful for any distraction from the strange world around her, and luckily, Tilly kept up enough conversation for the both of them.

"Have another drink, sugar."

She wrapped her fingers around the cool bottle Tilly offered. "Thanks." She didn't bring it to her lips but let her gaze roam around the bar. A cute blonde server laughed and joked with all the Disciples and the rest of the customers. Wren noticed that she tried to coax a smile out of Jennings, but he wore a stoic mask that even her flirtatious manner couldn't soften.

For some reason, that made Wren appreciate him even more. The hard man couldn't be buttered up with beer and winks, but several times she thought she'd seen his true self shine through with her.

Her attention swung to the door. A customer walked in. His blue jeans and flannel shirt marked him as an everyday joe rather than a member of the gang. When he walked up to the bar and talked to the bartender, Wren couldn't hear what was exchanged. But a minute later, the woman disappeared through a door and came out with a takeout bag.

The man turned away from the bar, took one step and then spun back.

"Wait a minute. I'm supposed to have four burgers, three fries. The bag feels light." He started to open the folded top of the bag.

Chairs scraped back and two men launched themselves at the customer. Several screams erupted from the ladies around Wren as the bikers tackled the man to the floor. One wrestled the bag out of his hand.

The guy let out a holler and threw a punch to defend himself, which earned him a fist to the eye.

Wren leaped to her feet at the first sight of blood. She pushed between the big bodies pinning the innocent man to the dusty floor.

"Stop!" she cried. "He's bleeding! Let me help him!"

She squeezed between men and dropped to her knees next to the injured man. The cut just beneath his brow wasn't a simple split. It looked like the guy who hit him wore a big knuckle ring that caused a lot of damage.

"I need a clean towel!" Her demand echoed in the abrupt silence.

A big black boot fell into her line of vision, and then the scent of the man she was beginning to know very well flooded her senses.

"Here." Jennings pressed a bar towel into her hand. She pressed it to the cut on the man's eye to staunch the flow of blood.

"I need a first-aid kit." She took in the man's face. His brows were pinched in pain, but he was still conscious at least. He still might have a concussion from being tackled. By her estimate, he also needed at least five stitches.

"He's going to need a trip to the ER. And a plastic surgeon if he doesn't want a scar on this eye." She made a rough noise of disgust. "What the hell were they thinking to shove him down and beat him up over a bag of takeout?"

When nobody answered her, she got the feeling that they all knew far more than she did. But she didn't care—she had a patient who needed medical attention.

She searched the man's face. "How are you feeling? Can you tell me your name?"

"Joey."

"Okay, Joey. I'm going to make sure you get bandaged up before you go to the hospital for stitches."

"I was just getting food for our game night," he mumbled.

She twisted her head to look at Jennings. "Call an ambulance. He could have a head injury from the fall."

Jennings's dark gaze captured hers. "Bad idea." Then he tore his stare from hers and looked around the bar. "Who here has a car to drive our friend to the hospital?"

Chapter Eight

Jennings switched on the light and closed the bedroom door. Wren stood just feet away, looking as lost and confused as she did when he announced that someone would drive the victim to the hospital rather than calling an ambulance.

He could guess what was inside that takeout bag, and it wasn't burgers and fries.

"I don't understand any of this." Wren shook her head with such despondence that it twisted his heart with a small pang. The wavy ends of her hair trailed across the tops of her breasts.

"Of course you don't understand." He took a step closer to her.

When he reached for her, she let him cup her face. God, even after all she'd been through, this woman still trusted him.

He should get her out of this place. Hide her.

He searched her pretty face. Her wide eyes spoke to all the shock she'd endured. As he stared at her, a flush warmed her cheeks.

"It's probably not a good idea to tell you why they tackled that guy in the bar."

"I'm guessing something was in that bag. What was it?"

He grunted. "I should have known you'd catch on. You're smart. Drugs are being moved through the bar."

Her jaw dropped.

"I've known for months. But this is the first time I've seen it. My guess is that guy was given the wrong bag."

She nodded. "If he'd opened it, he would have found drugs."

"That's right."

Pulling away from him, she walked across the room and sank to the edge of the bed. For several seconds she didn't move or speak. Then she bent to remove her shoes and set them aside on the carpet.

She looked so small. So beaten by her circumstances.

He removed his own boots and crossed the room to sit on the bed at her side.

"Everything is so complicated," she whispered.

"Yes."

"Except one thing." When she turned her head to look at him, his gut clenched hard at the look in her eyes.

His lips quirked at the corner. "What's that, honey?"

In a quick move, she threw herself into his lap, straddling him. "Us in this bed."

He didn't know how fast he could get an erection until that very moment. His stiff cock shoved against his fly.

"I have to know if the second time lives up to the first," she purred.

A growl burned up his throat as he trapped her pussy against his bulge with a palm on her ass. "The gauntlet is thrown…"

Her chest rose and fell in small pants. "Kiss me."

Everything in his body urged him to throw her down, spread those beautiful thighs and bury himself balls-deep.

The part of him that knew how damn frightened she'd been over the past two days took things slower.

Hooking his hand around her nape, he drew her in until their lips were a breath apart. "I can make you feel good, baby."

"Then do it." Her demand washed through him with a heat he rarely experienced. Desire clutched at his core.

At the same moment he nudged her pussy with his erection, he claimed her mouth. The kiss ripped a moan from her. She threw her arms around his neck, angled her head and kissed him back with more passion than he'd ever received from any of his past lovers.

Need consumed his mind. He threw himself into nibbling her lips until she begged for more. Then fed her his tongue with slow passes meant to send her to the breaking point.

He flicked his tongue across hers again and again. Easing her off his lap, he laid her on the mattress. When he settled his hand between her thighs, she bucked her hips and cried out.

She scrabbled at his shirt, only able to pull off one sleeve, so he stripped it off the rest of the way and stretched out on top of her.

Her luminous eyes blazed up at him. "Show me how good it can be, Jennings."

"I'll show you that and more." His harsh promise drew a squeak from her as he tore her clothes off and flipped her onto her stomach.

Her delicate fingers dug into the covers. Twisting her head to the side, she revealed that the blush she'd started with was now a red stain on one cheekbone. "Please," she panted.

"Oh yes, baby. You'll get what you ask for." He guided her hips off the bed. God, the tight globes of her ass had him aching and ready to blow.

He slipped his fingertips along the undercurve. She let out another soft moan that ended in a cry when he plunged his fingers into her tight, wet sheath.

"Fuck!" He lost himself to the noises she made as he drilled his fingers deep and then withdrew with a slow glide that said he was much more in control than he felt.

"Yesssss!" She pushed against his fingers when he sank them to the base of his hand again. Her pussy flooded. Juices soaked his hand.

He gained his knees behind her, thankful he had on his jeans. Without that barrier between them, he didn't know if he could stop himself from sinking into her bareback.

His balls clenched tight to his body at the thought of having her that way even as it scared the hell out of him. He never took a woman without protection.

This isn't any woman.

The thought hit his brain at the same moment she began to shudder. He fucked his fingers in and out of her even as he slid the other hand between her legs to stroke her clit.

A strangled sound burst out of her. She rocked into his hand.

"That's it, baby. Take what you need. What you want. Come for me."

His urging came out in guttural tones, but she understood. Her inner walls squeezed hard around his fingers, milking him.

Her release hit fast and furious. There was no muffling her scream of bliss, and his only regret was not being able to plunge his tongue into her mouth at the exact moment she let go.

So he did the next best thing.

He plunged his tongue into her clenching pussy.

* * * * *

Liquid heat encompassed Wren. The flames of need stretched on and on as Jennings licked her pussy while she continued to come. When he pulled his fingers free and replaced them with his talented tongue, she squeezed her eyes shut and stifled a scream of pleasure.

"Oh god! Yes!"

He thrust his tongue in, swirled it and drew out again. Her mind barely had time to catch up to the sensation before he slipped his tongue lower and lapped at her clit. Every nerve in her body tensed, hovering on the precipice of another orgasm.

"No!" she panted. "I want to come on your cock."

He drew his mouth from her slick folds, his primal growl all the answer she needed. She twisted her head to look at him as he worked off his jeans and slid a condom over his turgid cock. The head was purple and shiny in her peripheral, and then he was inside her.

Shoving deep.

Claiming every single inch of her body.

He cupped her breasts and thrust hard. Swishing the pads of his thumbs over her aching-hard nipples, he drove her to yet another level of need.

His hips slammed into her. The pressure of his cock deep inside her pulled moans from some dormant well.

"Fuck! Baby, I'm—" He bit back the word but she felt it.

His body shook. He rooted his cock deep and began fucking her in fast jerks.

Her pussy clamped on his thick length. The single contraction was all the warning he received before she was coming again, harder this time.

He pinched her nipples. Bit her throat. His fingers dug into her hips as he drove them to a final mind-numbing climax.

Pumping inside her two more times...then three...he sucked her earlobe between his teeth and gave it a sharp nip that heightened what she was already experiencing.

Her mind blanked. Slowly, she collapsed to the mattress, face down, unable to do more than stare at her lover's hard, gorgeous body as he moved to the bathroom to take care of the condom.

Oh yes. Round two was *just* as good—if not better than—the first.

She flipped onto her back, eyes closing on the little aftershocks of bliss zapping her system.

When she felt Jennings's weight on the bed, she opened her eyes to see him crawling in. His steely arm banded around her middle and he hitched her tight against him. His lips branded hers with a kiss so tender that it left her…stunned.

Who was this man really, when he wasn't acting like a big, tough biker?

After he broke the kiss, he smoothed the hair off her cheek. "How are you holding up, honey?"

She blinked at him. "I can't believe you're asking."

"Don't look so shocked. You've been through a lot." Again, he stroked a fingertip over her cheek.

Talking about her emotions while a man held her was completely new. The men she'd been with got out of bed and left immediately after the act was finished. And none of them gave a damn about her state of mind.

"It's been a lot to take in." She bit down on her bottom lip.

His stare shifted to her mouth. A crease appeared between his dark brows. "You're doing great."

She started to shake her head, but he trapped the point of her chin between his thumb and forefinger.

Holding her gaze, he insisted, "Yes, you *are*. You took care of your brother. You're helping me to stay undercover. Hell, you identified the guy who visited the home as the same one on the phone at the church. You should know how much that helps. We're still digging into the visitor's log and the surveillance from that day."

"It's my job to look and listen."

"You're smart enough to realize that something bigger was happening with that guy at the bar and the takeout bag."

"Because two guys tackled him! Over a burger!"

He trailed his finger over her lips, a silent reminder to keep her voice down. Then he followed the caress with another kiss. The soft stamp of his mouth melted her insides like warm syrup over a pat of butter.

When he drew back, their gazes connected. Suddenly shy, she ducked her head against his shoulder.

He held her close but didn't speak. Long minutes later, she said, "I can't believe I've slept next to you twice. And after sex too."

She felt the rhythm of his breathing change. "What do you mean?" he asked.

"I mean you didn't have to sleep beside me. Most guys leave. But I appreciate that you stay. I can't believe I'm saying this, but it makes me feel safer."

He swept his hand over her spine. "I'm not leaving you alone in this place, Wren. Or any other place."

Her gut tightened at the memory of what happened last time he walked away from her and that guy called Darius Dark yanked her down on his lap and started groping her.

As if understanding the direction of her thoughts, Jennings pressed his lips to her forehead. "Nothing like that will happen again. I promise."

Her insides juddered. "And what you said to that guy?"

He studied her face. "Which part?"

Her breaths came faster. "The 'my property' part."

For a heartbeat, his chest stopped moving. "I was just getting my point across to a guy who owns three brain cells."

She giggled. The dull expression on Darius Dark's face definitely indicated he wasn't the brightest bulb in the box.

She felt Jennings relax against her. He glided his hand down her back to cup her ass. Her amusement cut off, replaced by the hot ache of desire when he dipped his fingers low and gathered the juices left from her last orgasm.

Sinking her fingers into his shoulders, she levered herself upward and straddled him. "I hope that drawer's well-stocked with condoms."

His eyes crinkled with a bad-boy smile. "Oh, it is, baby."

"Good. Because I'm going to"—she leaned in, rubbing her bare breasts against his muscled chest—"ride your hard cock until I stop thinking."

He released his grip on her waist to snake out a hand for one of those condoms. "If you're looking for sex amnesia, I'm your guy."

Her laugh was throatier this time as she sucked on the side of his neck. "I have no doubt at all that you can handle me."

And anything else that comes up.

Chapter Nine

Jennings had been a light sleeper ever since his four older brothers got old enough to prank him.

They drew weird eyebrows with magic marker. They did the old tried-and-true shaving cream in the palm then tickle the nose trick. When the shaving cream hit his face, he'd startled out of a damn good dream. Of course, he no longer recalled the dream but he could still smell the pine scent of the cream.

A half-dozen other tricks were played on the baby of the family until he started rearing up in bed and scaring his brothers so bad they left skid marks in their tightey-whiteys. Now he practically slept with one eye open—nothing could get past him, especially within the walls of the Disciples' clubhouse.

So when Wren tried to ease out of bed without waking him, he latched on to her wrist.

She let out a gasp and twisted to look at him.

He searched her face. "God, you're lovely this morning."

Her lips, already parted with surprise, formed an O. Her eyelids hooded, showing off those long, natural lashes he'd noticed the first time he saw her.

The way she twisted to look at him, her hair tumbling over one shoulder, made her look like the muse of an artist.

He skimmed a finger down her thin side. If he had his way, he would get her out of this situation and then do everything possible to give her peace from the stress she suffered. To put a healthy glow in her cheeks and a few more pounds on her would become his number one goal—if he let it.

"Where are you going?" His voice came out a bit throatier than it did most mornings.

"To the shower. I have to be at work soon."

"I'll be ready to drive you."

She nodded and eased out of bed. He watched her hips sway as she padded across the room. Alone with him, she wasn't so edgy. He hated that he needed her to play this role, but it was the only way to keep her safe and him from being made after Viper's death.

Damn, her ass was a nice little handful. Thinking of closing his hands on it and pulling her down on his cock made his balls tighten with desire.

He needed to get a grip. His team would pick up on the changed vibe between him and Wren in a heartbeat.

Once the bathroom door closed, he reached for his phone.

He'd barely picked it up before it started vibrating with an incoming call. He glanced at the ID and swung his legs over the edge of the bed, at full alert.

"What's up?"

Lexis's gruff voice filled his ear. "I called to warn you."

"Great start to the day. Warn me about what?" He shot a glance at the closed bathroom door. At that moment, the shower started. He couldn't get distracted by the thought of hot water slicking over Wren's naked body but was relieved that the noise would muffle his conversation.

"The body was found."

Lexis's statement hardened his muscles to granite.

"Jesus Christ, man. Who did you send to clean up? We've never had this happen so quick."

"The guy hasn't been identified yet."

"It's only a matter of time before they figure it out."

"We're handling it."

Jennings grunted. The urge to bounce his leg and dispel some of his nerves burned, but he held still and controlled it. As the youngest brother, any tell would invite one of his brothers to start picking so it was a habit he'd learned to kick. He loved his brothers, but they could be assholes.

"Just lie low. Don't take any risks."

A familiar voice spoke up in the background. "That's like telling a volcano not to erupt. The *Titanic* not to sink."

The voice joining Lexis's was quieter for being in the background, but Jennings heard every single word. He was obviously on speakerphone.

He pushed a heavy sigh through his nostrils. "Julius."

"Jennings."

"Nobody needs your input on the matter."

"Just speaking the truth, bro. Last time you walked in here, you told us that you killed a man."

"I was protecting a woman." He ground the syllables through his teeth and stared at the closed bathroom door, willing said woman to stay in the shower a little longer.

"I'm muting you for a minute, Jennings."

The line went silent. Jennings could only guess that Lexis and Julius were exchanging a few heated words that they didn't want him to overhear.

When he came back on the line, Lexis said, "When is the next drug run?"

"No one shared the schedule with me. But based off what's been happening for months, I'd say three, four days at most."

"You've got to be on that run."

"I plan on it."

"We're working on an exit strategy. In the meantime, don't blow your cover. We need enough to take the Disciples down completely. There can be no way of rebuilding their club after this."

"The next run, I'll have all the evidence I need." He still had that listening device in place at the church. Unfortunately, it wasn't high-tech enough to transmit directly to the team. They'd learned the hard way once before that criminals were able to scan for the more advanced bugs. This cheap one flew under their radar, but it meant he had to retrieve it. Then he'd have even more evidence of what was going on.

"Can you make it three days without killing anybody else, brother?" Julius's remark came through loud and clear—and in a blink, Jennings was locked and loaded for battle.

He jerked to his full height, phone clamped to his ear, adrenaline flowing through his veins. "If you were here right now, you'd be wearing two black eyes and fewer teeth."

His brother's laugh was that old teasing one he knew from their childhood. "That's the spirit, Jennings. You know I've got your back, right? We might argue, but it never lasts long."

He wasn't feeling so warm and fuzzy. "Maybe someday I'll hold a grudge a lot longer," he bit off.

"Enough." Like a father figure, Lexis put a stop to their bickering. Something that irritated Jennings even more.

A crash from beyond the bedroom walls, deeper in the club, made him grab his shirt off the floor. "I gotta go. Something's going down."

The commotion continued, more noises of items breaking reaching him. He'd heard enough bodies fall to know one when he heard one.

He ended the call and threw on his clothes. With the phone shoved in his back pocket, he hurried out of the room.

About ten people gathered around somebody on the floor. All Jennings could see was a set of boots sticking out from between the onlookers.

He was taller than most men in the club, and he used that to his advantage to see into the huddle. Blood pooled on the wood floor.

"Fuck, what happened here?" he asked the guy beside him.

"He's been shot!" one of the ladies cried out.

Everyone started talking at once. Jennings pushed his way into the fray and knelt beside the victim. His pale skin was slick with sweat. The stench of blood and gunpowder clung to him.

"Somebody find the doc!" a person called.

"I already called him when Matthews staggered through the door and collapsed." The woman that Wren had gotten chummy with the day before hovered over the fallen man. If Jennings recalled correctly—and he always did—Matthews had taken Tilly to bed more than a handful of times.

Another person leaning over Matthews held out a wad of bar towels, probably none of which were clean let alone sterile. "What about the vet? He can stop the bleeding."

A familiar voice stopped all chatter and speculation dead. Kojak, the president of the Disciples, hadn't been in residence for a few days. Nobody knew where he'd gone but the VP, and Jennings never could get him to talk so he didn't bother to try. Easier to pry intel out of the rest of the club.

Kojak stepped into the ring of people. "The vet can't be reached either."

Jennings didn't like the way he stated that, his tone flat and cold.

"Get Matthews onto the table."

As a few guys reached for the man's limbs and hefted him up, a sharp cry carried across the room. The sound rippled the hair on Jennings's forearms, and he automatically swung his head to look for *her*.

Wren.

She shoved through the bikers. Determination blazed on her face.

She nudged aside more than a few whores to reach the middle of the room. Her hands fisted, her gaze locked on the dying man.

She whipped her head around and gave Jennings a piercing stare that told him just how dire Matthews's situation was.

123

"I need all the first-aid kits you've got in the club. Ladies, I need towels—clean ones. And hot water. Anybody who's not fetching me supplies can clear out!"

* * * * *

Wren took in the situation. The shooting victim was losing blood fast.

"Call an ambulance!"

Nobody reached for their phone. They all stared at her like the imposter she was.

Jennings stepped up beside her. "We can't risk the police reports. Can you do anything for him?"

"I'll try, but—" She threw her hands in the air. "I need a clean sheet for underneath him. Didn't I just see people fucking on this table last night?"

"I'll get one!" Tilly whirled and ran to fetch the sheet.

Several first-aid kits landed on the table next to Matthews.

"Tell me what you need," Jennings said.

"Gloves. Gauze. Scissors. All of it." She looked up at Tilly, who arrived with the sheet in hand. "Can you cut off his shirt?"

"Y-yes."

Wren gave her a sharp look. "If you can't, somebody else will."

"I'll do it." She took up the scissors that Jennings handed her and slowly began to cut the blood-soaked fabric off his body.

"Does she know what she's doing?" someone whispered.

"She said she's a nurse."

Ignoring the talk about her, Wren waited for Tilly to finish cutting the shirt off the man before directing two men to lean him onto his good side far enough for the woman to slip the sheet beneath him.

After they followed her orders, she moved close to examine the wound.

"What's this man's name?" she demanded.

"Matthews."

She leaned over him. "Matthews, I'm Wendy. I'm going to help you, okay?"

The fact that he wasn't responding to her wasn't surprising, but it *was* alarming.

She began dabbing away the blood so she could see just how bad the wound was. To her relief, the bullet had entered a part of his body that didn't have any vital organs.

She sought out Jennings. "Can you lift him again? I need to see his back."

As soon as Jennings gripped Matthews and tilted him on one side, the man issued a low groan.

"Good. The bullet exited through his back. I won't need to go digging for it. We need painkillers. What can you find for me?" she asked Tilly.

Around the club, she wasn't surprised that a bunch of prescription drug bottles hit the table in front of her or by the handful of pills pulled out of somebody's pocket.

She nodded to Jennings. "Get two pills out of that first bottle and make him swallow them." She held the gauze over the bleeding wound.

When somebody handed Jennings a bottle of whiskey for Matthews to wash them down with, Wren made a noise. Mixing drugs and alcohol was a terrible idea, but it would be a miracle if the patient didn't die of sepsis from the infection surely setting in from the hole blown in his side.

After he swallowed the pills and chased them with whiskey, she set about cleaning out the wound.

The minute she dumped antiseptic on his side, he reared off the table, fists swinging. Jennings hooked an arm around her middle and yanked her back just before Matthews struck her. But she felt the air wave across her face.

He collapsed on the table again, and she continued to work, meticulously cleaning both the entry point and the exit wound. As she focused on the task, she sank her teeth into her lower lip in concentration.

Tilly stood a few feet away, arms wrapped around her stomach, tears streaming down her face. "Do you really know what you're doing?"

Wren pushed out a sigh but didn't glance away from her work. "I was in medical school."

Silence pervaded the club. She could hear one of those pills drop if somebody knocked one off the table.

She went on. "I ended up being an LPN because I couldn't finish. The nursing home paid. They provided training in exchange for a two-year contract. But that's up in two months. Then I won't be tied to that job and I can finish med school. If I want..." She trailed off, fighting to keep the emotion out of her voice.

She never could stop her feelings from invading whenever she thought about the sacrifices she'd made.

Jennings edged closer to her. The heat from his body and the solid wall of muscle provided strength she needed without him ever touching her.

When her gaze met his, several thoughts played through her mind. One being that she wanted to help those in need, and that meant working in an area that other medical workers refused to.

She always dreamed of working in a clinic like the one they'd driven past in East Canon. The poor area must need help. Help she could provide. Maybe someday she could make a difference there. Do some good in the world.

"Bandage." She held out a hand to Jennings.

He tore open the packet and she took the gauze between her gloved fingers, applying it to the wound.

"Tape."

He tore a strip off the roll and passed that to her too. When she had one wound patched up, she looked at the men still left standing. Those who could stomach the sight of all that blood and her probing around in the wound for this long gave her looks of respect.

"Roll him on his side again. He passed out, and that's good, because what I need to do to that exit wound won't feel good."

She glanced up at Jennings. In the depths of his dark eyes, she saw respect mingled with something else she couldn't put a name to.

After long minutes of cleaning and using all the supplies on hand to close up the larger wound on the victim's back, Wren stepped away from the table. She was exhausted, wrung out from her nerves...

And completely happy.

She met Jennings's stare. All at once, she recognized what it was that she saw in his eyes.

Admiration.

Chapter Ten

Wren stripped off the latex gloves and dropped them into the wastebasket. Though Jennings saw the fatigue etched on her face—along with a big measure of concern—her shoulders were thrust back and her head held high.

"He still needs a hospital," she announced to those left in the room. Many had run out at the first sight of blood and several more during her patching up Matthews.

She swung her gaze to Kojak. He stood a few feet away from the table where the patient lay, knocked out from the pills and booze he'd swallowed.

"He needs antibiotics. Can you get them?" Her tone had several people sucking in breaths of shock.

Jennings took a swift step forward, prepared to die on this hill for Wren in the event the president of the Disciples took offense to her challenge.

Kojak cocked an eyebrow at Jennings. Then he gave a single nod. "We'll get some."

He spotted the warning in the prez's eyes. Right now, he had to heed it or lose his tenuous position in the club's favor.

Holding out a hand to Wren, Jennings shot her a quelling look that made her small chin jut in reaction.

Before she could say or do anything else to jeopardize them, he led her out of the room. As soon as they hit the hallway leading to the room they'd laid claim to, she tugged at his hand.

"That man can't stay on the table. Those idiots need instruction—"

Shutting her up was the only thought in his mind at that moment. If the Disciples heard her calling them idiots, they'd take offense and send her packing—and him with her.

He cupped her face and slammed his lips over hers. At first contact, she stiffened. Then melted.

Her mouth softened under his. He dragged in a deep breath of air, thinking to pull her sweet, perfumed essence into his head. Instead, his nostrils pinched at the scent of the blood coating her.

He broke the kiss and wordlessly hauled her the rest of the way to the bedroom. As soon as he closed and locked the door behind them, he strode to the bathroom and switched on the shower.

She drifted to the doorway, staring down at her blood-soaked shirt. She hesitated only a blink before stripping the shirt off and dropping it to the floor. Her jeans followed.

As she hooked her thumbs in the sides of her panties, she froze and met his gaze. "I'm late for work!"

"You just did your work, baby. Get in the shower."

"I can't just call off. I need that money to pay for Danny's rehab!"

"I'll cover it."

She gaped at him.

His lips twisted. "Guess I found another way to keep you from talking."

Her eyes flashed bright with anger. "You kissed me to shut me up."

"And I'll do it again. But Wren, I need you to play better with these guys. You stick out too much. I need you to blend in to keep my cover. Can you do that?"

She stared at him. A red flush climbed her throat. "I'm sorry. I didn't realize that I'm blowing it."

"I asked you to help Matthews. But the Disciples expect everyone—especially women—to keep quiet and do as ordered."

She nodded. "I understand. I'll do better. I don't want to put you in jeopardy."

Unable to just stand there and not touch the half-naked woman, he took her by the upper arms. "Make no mistake—I wanted to kiss you. I *want* to kiss you. All the time. But we have to guard what we say, and I couldn't risk you offending somebody in the club. I'm close, Wren. So damn close I can feel the steel of the handcuffs I'll slap on their wrists."

He raised one as if she could see them too.

"And when I say I'll cover your brother's rehab, I mean if the FBI doesn't pay for it, then I'll transfer a fat sum to the facility."

After a long heartbeat, she nodded. "I get it. You'll do anything for this case."

He stared down at the top of her bowed head. The struggle burning his chest wasn't one he'd experienced before, and he'd done a hell of a lot in his twenty-eight years.

There weren't words to explain why he felt the bone-deep need to take care of her—in all ways.

Shower steam swirled in the air around them. Gently, he stripped off her bra and finally her panties. Just seeing the cleft between her thighs had his cock gripping to pound into her. Or better, to drag his tongue up and down that slippery seam until she forgot all her cares.

With a gentle nudge, he guided her into the shower and closed the door.

Brought to life by the hot spray of water, she twisted away from the door and let it wash over her. The blood she wore from the battle she fought would run down the drain.

And fight she had. To keep a stranger she didn't even know alive.

But in turn, she'd given away too much. No longer was she able to fade into the background of the club as one of the girls. When she talked of her pursuit of medicine, everyone heard her. They took into account that she wasn't one of them.

He needed to speak to Lexis right away. An exit strategy was already forming in his head, a way to get Wren out of here and to safety.

But it means she goes without me.

The thought stopped him in his tracks, one foot over the threshold between bathroom and bedroom.

He grabbed his phone and shot off a text to Lark, telling her that Wren needed clothes.

Lark responded within seconds and then dropped an address for him to pick them up. He calculated the distance to the spot. He wouldn't have time to run there and back before she was finished with her shower, but he'd put her on his bike and make a few loops through town to ensure none of the Disciples tracked his movements.

He lowered the phone just as the water stopped. Drawn to the woman on the other side of that door, he edged closer, listening.

When the soft cry hit his eardrums, he burst through the door.

Wren jerked around, towel slipping on her bare breasts that glistened with water drops.

His stare snapped to her face. Her brows were creased but she was dry-eyed.

"What are you doing?" She drew the towel over her breasts, banning him from the sumptuous line of cleavage.

"I thought you were crying."

She stared at him. "I'm not crying. You heard me stub my toe on the damn vanity."

He directed his gaze to her feet. One small toe was pinker than the rest.

"Are you all right?"

"It's fine. I'm just clumsy sometimes, especially when I'm under stress. I hurry too much and I—" She broke off. "Why are you looking at me like that?"

He had no clue what the hell his face looked like, but he could tell from the throb in his chest that it wasn't something he could explain.

Like how he wanted to pick her up and cradle her against his chest to keep her safe even from stubbing her toe.

Slowly, he moved toward her. When he clamped his hands on her waist, the moist terrycloth warmed his skin. Knowing that the thin fabric was the only barrier between his lips and every naked inch of Wren's flesh didn't help the throb in his cock.

He lifted her onto the vanity top. Her big blue eyes were soft pools as he took hold of her ankle and raised her foot so he could examine her toe.

"It's not broken."

"I think I'd know if it were." Her tone was haughty.

He brushed his thumb tenderly over the digit. "Of course you would. You're trained."

She dipped her head. "Not completely. I never made it to the practical work with patients. Everything I know came from a book or experience in the nursing home."

He eyed her. Beautiful and smart. Caring beyond measure. She made sacrifices for not only her brother but that total stranger she just saved from slowly bleeding out because the Disciples couldn't risk the investigation into a gunshot wound.

"How are you single?" He studied her beautiful face from the hair waving off her forehead to the point of her small chin.

She shook her head. "Why are you asking me that?"

"It's a valid question. You're smart and skilled and stunning."

A flush climbed her throat—and extended downward to the tops of her breasts pressing against the towel too.

"I dated a few guys in college, but their egos couldn't hold up to me getting better grades. Medical school was the same way. I was genuinely interested in a few guys, but they took everything I said as a challenge."

"A real man is never going to be intimidated by a real woman."

Her stare fixed on his. A beat of silence throbbed between them.

"Men want to be dominant. Controlling." She dashed her tongue over her lower lip.

"Weak men feel that need. Not every man is like that."

When he slipped his fingers under the edge of the towel cinched around her breasts, she leaned back. The resistance tugged the towel free, and it dropped to reveal her beautiful body.

Groaning, he cupped her breasts and captured her mouth. She whimpered, and he swept his tongue over hers. The pounding need inside him to lay claim to this woman, ravish her from top to bottom and every supple curve in between, stole his mind.

He settled his hands on her ass—and yanked her past the vanity, into his hardening cock.

* * * * *

Wren ground her pussy into Jennings's bulge. God, she'd never needed to be touched so badly. Her insides fluttered with want. Each pass of his tongue in her mouth sent electric tingles through her limbs.

When he lifted her, the towel dropped to the floor. As she wrapped her arms around his neck, her breasts brushed his chest. The cool leather of his cut sent a forbidden thrill to her core.

Her pussy flooded, and by the time he lay her on the bed, she was on the verge of begging for him to fill her with his thick cock.

He straightened away from her, staring down at her body like a hungry animal. "Spread your legs, baby."

A sharp pang of desire struck and she slowly let her thighs fall apart.

"Spread your pussy for me to see all that slick wetness."

Her breaths came in rough pants. Oh god. His heated words made her even wetter. Men only made demands like this in adult videos.

He didn't look like he was kidding. That dark blaze in his eyes set her on fire.

Hands trembling, she eased her hand between her legs and used two fingers to part her lips. Air rushed over her soaked folds, and her pussy clenched once as if pleading for him to finish this torment.

He let out a low groan and stripped off his vest, then his shirt. Chiseled muscles bulged as if he was holding himself back from taking her hard and fast.

"Dip one finger inside your pussy."

Her lips parted on a rasp. Could she perform such an intimate act in front of somebody?

Her lover was asking—no, commanding.

Keeping her gaze steady on his face, she breeched her opening with her fingertip...then sank it slowly in to the first knuckle.

Jennings ripped open his fly. When he pulled out his stiff cock, gleaming with precum, she moaned and filled her pussy with her finger.

"Fuck yes, baby. Finger your pussy and think about me sliding my cock into you."

Need blasted through her body as she obeyed his command and watched him strip down to the buff.

Again and again, she plunged her finger inside her needy pussy. When he had a condom in place, he positioned his body between her legs and gripped her by the hips. He leaned in close enough to kiss her.

His stare burned into hers. "Let me lick off your finger."

Her eyes squeezed shut at the hot command, and a moan burst from her as she lifted her hand and he swallowed her finger.

His swollen cock head was poised at the root of her. With his hot mouth enveloping her finger and sucking off her juices, he filled her in a swift thrust.

She locked her hips around his waist and angled her body to meet him. As he sank deep, his balls rocked forward to brush her ass.

They shared a moan, and he released her finger to take her mouth instead. His hungry kisses stole all her worries and anxiety.

She threw her entire focus into the man filling her with unspeakable pleasure. She dug her fingers into the muscles layered on his spine. She drove into his every thrust and kissed him back with abandon.

Everything about her situation confused and scared her. Everything but this.

Jennings was good and honest, safe and raw. She didn't need to pretend to be something she wasn't with him—he *saw* her.

That never happened, and she got the feeling that after they parted ways, it never would again.

When he grabbed her leg and lifted it to rest on his shoulder, the new angle threw her body into overdrive. Her pussy strangled his length. Hard throbs deep in her core came faster and faster. Her muffled cry was stolen by his lips and tongue.

As he stroked his thumb over her clit, her nerves shattered into a million pieces. She came with a hard pulse. Her clit throbbed. Her mind floated on ecstasy.

Jennings issued a low growl. His spine tensed under her fingers. With one swift shove, he let go with her. His body twitched as he poured his hot cum inside her. The pressure in her core increased as she realized just how much she wanted this man and every drop he had to give her.

His chest heaved, and he dropped his forehead against hers, breathing hard. "I never want to leave this bed."

The admission did something to her. It jogged her heart.

He nuzzled her nose with his own. "What have you done to me?" His whisper rushed over her lips.

What had *she* done? What was *he* doing to *her*?

But she couldn't lose touch with herself or lose sight of her goal to protect her brother and get him clean. She needed to escape this mess with the biker gang, and after it was all over, she'd leave Spring Valley. Maybe she could work at another nursing home in another town while she completed her medical degree.

She didn't have time for emotional entanglements.

"Lark, Dove and Avalynn warned me about you," she said.

He levered his body off hers to stare into her eyes. "What did they warn you about?"

"They warned me not to fall. That you're fling material. Not to get serious."

His lips tightened but only for a second. Slowly, he withdrew from her body and rolled to the side. "Historically speaking, that would be correct. But that's history."

She focused on what he was telling her.

"The present and future can change."

When he twisted his head and pierced her in his stare, her heart tumbled even further.

This man could steal her heart and make her lose sight of everything...but hardening herself against Jennings was impossible.

She didn't have any weapons in her arsenal for that fight.

Chapter Eleven

The nursing home doors opened and two middle-aged women walked out. One made a comment about the beautiful flowers flanking the entrance, and then they walked to their car.

Jennings stood off to the side, watching all the activity. He didn't have a reason to be lurking around. He really didn't have any reason to be concerned for Wren's safety, but when the urge struck to swing by her workplace, it was too strong to ignore. He'd learned long ago not to let any of his instincts go unnoticed, so here he was.

A lanky guy in a hoodie loped across the parking lot. As he approached, Jennings heard him muttering to himself, too low for him to make out the words. He studied the guy's face before he entered the building.

Again, a strong pull to go inside and follow the kid was a guiding force he couldn't ignore. He pushed away from the building and followed him.

After the kid cleared the front desk security, Jennings stopped to give his false name and say he was stopping to give his girlfriend her keys she forgot at home. The clerk gave him a sticker name tag, and he plastered it onto his T-shirt.

The crew was sleeping off yet another heavy party in honor of Matthews surviving his wounds. Since not much was going on around the clubhouse, Jennings didn't see the point in sticking around watching people sleep or fuck. In the time he was gone, he didn't foresee anybody making a drug run. Besides, he was in now — they'd call him to ride along.

Trailing the kid through a few corridors, he listened hard, trying to catch whatever he was muttering. The words came in short bursts. Either he was crazy, distraught or high. After seeing his face, he'd lay bets on the last.

The chain on his belt rattled, and he lightened his footsteps so his boots didn't thump so loud or draw more attention than he was already getting from the nursing home staff, patients and visitors.

Unless he was with his team or his brothers, Jennings was almost always the tallest guy in the room. He garnered a lot of attention too, especially dressed in the black leather that made him stand out in this town as the bad guy. Hell, maybe even evil.

When they drew close to a medical cart full of supplies sitting in the hallway, the kid veered left toward it. He slowed down, looking over the contents. One finger twitched aside some bandages, but he didn't take anything.

Jennings went on full alert. The kid was definitely sketchy, from his behavior to his actions. He continued tracking him to the end of the hallway, where he turned right into another wing of the sprawling nursing home. He'd been told by a security guard that Wren worked with the patients in this ward.

Swinging his head left and right, he searched for her. She wasn't standing in plain sight, but more people were sitting in the hallway on chairs or in wheelchairs. A housekeeping worker arranged carts of linens and several people were changing the bed sheets in various rooms as he passed.

The odor of disinfectant and something sour hung in the air, giving him an even bigger appreciation for Wren's strong character. Caring for people in this stage of life wasn't easy.

Ahead of him, the kid turned to enter a room. Jennings hung back.

"Hi, Grandpa."

A faint, thready voice responded.

"It's Ethan."

"Oh?"

"Your grandson."

Maybe Jennings had jumped to conclusions about the guy and he wasn't sketchy at all. He'd walked on the darker side of life for so long that everybody looked suspicious to him until they proved otherwise.

Then he heard another voice. One that sent a thrill through his core.

"Hi, Ethan. We haven't seen you around here for a few weeks." Wren's clear, high voice was a fresh breeze to his senses, blowing away the odor of suffering.

"I've been busy," Ethan said.

"Well, it's nice to see you. I'm sure your grandfather appreciates your visits. Isn't that right, Mr. Craig?"

The man replied too low for Jennings to hear.

"I'll be right back with your lunch tray and your afternoon medications."

Jennings dodged around the corner before Wren could spot him. She would probably give him hell for being here and he didn't want to disrupt her workday with the dark cloud of the situation she was in.

Footsteps moved away. Minutes passed and then he heard Wren again. "Here's your food, Mr. Craig. Meatloaf and mashed potatoes—one of your favorites. And your pills. Take these first and then I can check off that you've taken them."

"Oh, I can make certain my grandpa takes his medication." Ethan's voice drew Jennings around the corner.

"I'm sure you're great at taking care of your grandpa, but it's my job to make sure he takes his pills."

"I said I'll do it."

Jennings's fists knotted at his sides. Both Ethan's tone and the fact he was using it on Jennings's woman had red sparks of irritation flying through his head.

"Again, I appreciate your dedication to his care, but it's my job." Wren spoke with a little more emphasis, an indication that she wasn't happy about the way he spoke to her either.

"I haven't seen my grandpa in weeks. You can go now."

"Not until he takes his pills in front of me."

"I don't know what you're worried about. Are you calling me incompetent?"

"Look, Ethan, I already told you that I know you have your grandpa's best interests in mind. But *this* is my job. Mr. Craig, please take your pills for me."

"You're all jerks in this place! This is why I don't come here!" Ethan's heavy footsteps clomped. In a second, he reached the door and took off down the hall toward the exit.

Jennings didn't hesitate to follow. As soon as the kid made it out of the building, he grabbed him by the scruff of the neck and threw him against the wall. Ethan let out a squawk of surprise but the glare he fixed on Jennings was all tough guy.

"You were out of line in there, kid," Jennings bit out.

"Who the hell are you and why are you butting into my business?"

"You wanted the nurse to leave so you could take your grandpa's drugs, didn't you?"

145

"You don't know anything, man." He struggled in Jennings's hold and took a swing at him.

Jennings just pinned him to the wall and delivered a cuff to the ear that would ring his bell and followed up with a sock to the midsection meant to knock the air out of him without causing real damage.

"Unless you actually come here to see your grandpa instead of looking for a fix, don't come back. Got it?"

The kid sucked in a deep breath to fill his lungs again.

Jennings gave him another little shake and then shoved him toward the parking lot. "Go. And next time you talk to nurses that way, you'd better be looking over your shoulder. Because I'll be right behind you."

Ethan staggered away, picking up speed as he went.

Jennings watched him until he got in his beat-up car and drove off. He considered going inside to check on Wren, but she'd handled herself with all the professional poise he'd come to expect from her.

She would make it to the end of her shift. Then he'd put her on the back of his bike and take her out for a night on the town. During the brief call to his team, he'd made plans to meet them all in Denver for a small celebration. Livingston's birthday would definitely have them all unwinding in style. Being

146

with his team felt like his momma calling all her sons to the table for one of their big family dinners.

When Wren finally emerged from the building, he was there to slide his arm around her. Pulling her against him, finally, after that asshole kid harassed her, brought on a peace and calm that Jennings never expected.

He led her to his bike and handed her his helmet.

Her beautiful gaze lifted to his. "When are you going to buy yourself one of these?" She strapped it on.

Staring at her, he brushed his thumb over her plump lips. "Does that mean you're here to stay?"

* * * * *

Jennings's question tumbled through Wren's mind over and over again. As soon as she thought it would land, it took flight again like a leaf on the breeze.

The feel of his big, hard body in front of her didn't provide the right kind of distraction, either. Every turn they took on the road, each curve they leaned into together, amped up her libido even more.

By the time she saw the sign for Denver and realized they were taking that exit, the engine was too loud for her to ask why they were going to the city. She didn't have much choice now, did she? Jennings was in control—and if she were honest, she needed that.

Someone to make decisions for a while, to give her a break. The hum of the tires on the road and growl of the engine soothed her to a state of mind where she could examine some of the things that bothered her most.

She hoped Danny was faring well in rehab. The fact that he hadn't called her asking for a ride home was a huge step in the right direction. She hadn't anticipated him trying so hard, but it seemed that witnessing a murder was just what he needed to scare him straight.

Her mind shifted to the altercation with a patient's grandson this afternoon. She knew a person who was jonesing for a fix when she saw one. That kid's only interest in his grandfather lay in what painkillers he received.

Wren wasn't born yesterday — she was not letting him get his fix under her watch. The event made her question how many times he'd swindled one of the other nurses into walking away so he could swallow those pills.

She'd stood her ground even though her insides shook. As soon as he left, she'd nearly broken down thanks to the devastated look on Mr. Craig's face. He probably wasn't completely aware of what happened, but he didn't want his loved one to leave either.

By the time she looked up and saw the cityscape, she was more than ready for a change of scenery. She'd pondered enough heavy stuff for one day—

hell, for a lifetime. She was young and deserved whatever fun that Jennings had in store for her.

At least she hoped it was fun.

She chewed on her lip and held onto his waist tighter. What if this had something to do with the Disciples? After all, he hadn't told her their plans…only asked if she was there to stay.

The mere idea of being with a man like Jennings long-term scared her. There was so much she didn't know about him. So much that she could be wrong about.

But the way he looked at her, with his dark brown eyes melting her into a puddle, and the swipe of his thumb over her bottom lip left her with a deep ache of desire.

Her heart was involved now — and that terrified her even more. All the people close to her were gone. Even Danny hadn't been in her life in a meaningful way for a very long time.

Jennings turned into the parking lot of a restaurant that looked pretty upscale. Compared to the cheap fare she was accustomed to, this place was a big departure from the norm.

He rolled into a parking spot and cut the engine. When his hand covered hers where she still gripped his waist, her eyes closed on the sensation of being cared for by someone.

She released her hold on him and slid off the bike first, allowing him to swing his leg off the bike too.

He steadied her with a hand on her hip while she removed the helmet.

Suddenly, the back door of the SUV parked beside them whipped open. She threw herself into Jennings's arms, and he tucked her head against his chest with his fingers splayed over her skull.

"It's all right, baby. It's just my team."

Her nerves brought on a shiver even as embarrassment seeped in. "I'm so jumpy."

"It's my fault—I should have told you the plan."

She twisted to look at the open door. The perky little redhead standing there threw her a wave. "Hi, Wren."

She let out a low sigh and attempted a smile. "Hi, Lark." She glanced at Jennings. "It would be good to hear about that plan now."

He chuckled. "We're here for a birthday celebration."

Dismay filled her. "This place looks fancy. I'm in nurse's scrubs."

Lark's grin widened. "Don't worry—I guessed that this knucklehead wouldn't think about how you were dressed, so I brought something for you. If you'll just step into my portable dressing room..." She waved at the open door.

Wren tossed a look at Jennings.

"Go ahead, baby. I'll be talking to the guys."

At that moment, the rest of the doors opened and people piled out of the SUV. More doors opened in the black sports car on the other side of them, and Julius climbed out, looking sharp in black dress pants and a black button-down shirt. Avalynn got out too, looking as stunning as always.

With no more arguments in her, Wren climbed into the back of the SUV with Lark.

A garment bag hung there, unzipped to display a black dress.

"This will be an easy change, I promise. Take off your top." Lark's no-nonsense attitude sent Wren into action.

She slipped off her top and Lark helped her glide the dress overhead. "What is Jennings doing while I change clothes?"

"He's changing too. Didn't you see him get in the back of the car? Now kick off the shoes."

She did and pulled off her socks too, stuffing them inside the shoes. She shimmied her pants down her hips and off, then wiggled the dress down.

"Twist around and I'll zip you up."

She obeyed. "Is this how Sentry always operates?"

Lark laughed. "You'd be surprised at the situations we get into."

"You seem to know just what to do all the time. I'm such a mess compared to you."

"Oh, honey. You're just trying to survive. Nobody expects you to be perfect, Wren. You already have the perfect name."

"I don't know what that means."

Lark produced a hairbrush from the bag and set to work pulling the ponytail holder out of Wren's hair. "Remember? You have the bird name. You fit in with us."

"You also told me that Jennings is a player. He's fling material."

"Yes, but I was wrong."

The brush working over her scalp sent prickles of pleasure through her. "How do you know you were wrong?"

"Because I saw the way he looked at you just now. And the way he shielded you when you jumped? Lordy, that man is built for loving a woman. He just didn't know it until now."

Stunned, Wren could only blink at Lark as she finished brushing her hair. She used the brush to curl the ends and arranged her hair over her shoulders. Then she pulled out some makeup.

As she worked, she talked about the baby and how her back ached and kept her up at night, but Lexis rubbed her muscles until she could fall asleep again.

At that story, Wren experienced a sharp pang. To have what Lark did—a loving man and a family— was one of Wren's dreams. She'd never said it aloud, and she'd never told a soul how much she longed for a family of her own after going without one.

Of course, she had to get through med school first. Only after she had that degree in hand would she be able to settle down. By then, Jennings would be long gone from her life, the tenuous ties between them cut.

When Lark declared that she looked "stunning," she climbed out of the SUV to find every person from Sentry staring at her.

Only one gaze mattered.

Dressed in all black with a black cowboy hat, Jennings stepped up to her. He lifted a hand to her face...and all Wren could see was the emotion that Lark claimed to see too.

That man was built for loving.

And God help her, she did.

Chapter Twelve

The massive platter with a sizzling steak sat before every member of the Sentry team at the table and more than a few of the women too. The long table was brimming with food and drink. The bread baskets had been refilled twice while they were waiting on their meals. But three pregnant women and a bunch of hungry men could destroy some food, especially when it was good.

Jennings wrapped his fingers around his beer and raised it. "To Livingston. Sixty-two looks nice on you."

Laughter broke out, but Livingston shot him a flat look. "You know I'm in my forties."

"And it looks amazing on you, babe!" Dove leaned over to kiss his cheek.

Their private party was in a small space at the back of the restaurant. Despite a wall shielding them from the rest of the place, the strains of a live country music band and the stomp of dancers wearing boots still made them raise their voices to be heard.

Everybody lifted their drinks and toasted the birthday boy. Then they fell on their food like hungry wolves. Jennings had devoured half of this Delmonico before he noticed that Wren wasn't eating.

Neither was Avalynn. The pair seemed to be deep in conversation. Avalynn caressed her small baby bump. Jennings gave Julius a sharp look of concern with a nod toward his sister-in-law.

Julius leaned in to say something to her, and she gave him a distracted nod before continuing her conversation with Wren. Jennings tuned in to their discussion.

"You could try some teas for the nausea," Wren was telling Avalynn. She reached out and pulled the woman's water glass a bit closer to her. "Try sipping something often."

"Thanks, Wren. The other ladies stopped suffering from pregnancy nausea months ago, and I'm still living through it."

Jennings eyed Wren. She was so giving with her time, but she could use a fattening meal too. He plucked a thick slice of homemade bread from the basket, slathered it in butter and held it out to her.

She took it with a smile that lit up her eyes. Watching her bring the soft crust to her lips and nibble at it gave him pleasure.

In fact, taking care of her filled him with a warmth he never experienced before.

Looking around the table at Lexis, Livingston and Julius, he noted the way each man doted on his significant other. Lexis and Livingston were engaged in a lively conversation, but Lexis still reached over to rest his big hand on Lark's belly and the child they'd created.

Jennings focused on Wren. An overwhelming urge to stake his claim on her bubbled inside him.

He was...

No, that couldn't be.

It was too soon to fall in love with her.

But he knew the important things about her — her core of steel, her drive and fortitude. Her sweet nature shone through to the people she cared for. And the sexy woman who demanded that he pleasure her was a whole other dimension to her.

He could almost feel her arms around him as they leaned into the curves on his bike. From the beginning, she'd placed her trust in him. They'd placed trust in each other.

The fate of the op that he'd spent months working on lay in her hands. One word from her would put his life in jeopardy.

When he glanced up from his plate, he caught Lark staring at him. Understanding flashed in her eyes.

Don't say anything to her.

As if she heard the telepathic transmission, she gave a light shake of her head. The sympathy in her gaze felt like a lifeline too.

Damn, he didn't know how to love her. Loving his brothers, parents and extended family was very different from being *in* love.

He edged his hand across the tablecloth until his pinky brushed Wren's.

She glanced up, expression startled. Then she extended her pinky and stroked his in return.

His heart surged. He was pretty sure Lark twisted her head away before he could see her smug smile.

It was far from what he wanted to share with Wren, but he'd bide his time.

He dug into his steak and Wren ate too. Even Avalynn managed to have some salad and bread.

After the server cleared away their empty plates, a big chocolate cake was brought in.

"Four tiers for four decades, my amazing husband!" Dove got out of her seat to video Livingston blowing out the candles while Lexis joked about a bonfire.

Following a thick slice of the decadent treat, Jennings pushed away from the table. He held out a hand to Wren. "Dance with me."

Her jaw dropped. "You dance?"'

Julius let out a hoot and clapped his hands. "You haven't seen dancing until you've witnessed Jennings kickin' it up."

Casting a grin, Jennings clasped Wren by the hand and tugged. "Come and find out."

She looked at Avalynn and mouthed: *Oh my god!*

"Go! When a hot guy wants to dance with you, you go!" Avalynn shooed her off with a flick of her napkin.

With another yank, he hauled Wren to her feet. A laugh bubbled out of her, one of the first he'd ever heard. Spurred on by the sound, he led her to the main part of the restaurant.

Live music and dancers had the place hopping. Sentry had chosen this place for its distance from Spring Valley and also East Canon, but seeing the bar packed with people made him a little on edge.

He covertly scanned the patrons for black leather or the Disciples patch. He'd changed into nicer clothes and fit in with the crowd but that didn't mean he couldn't be recognized. Seeing no cause for concern, he pulled Wren forward.

He drew her right into the crowd. The country tune had the floor shaking with people stomping their boots in sync.

"Jennings! I can't dance like this!"

He tossed her a look over his shoulder. "I got you, baby."

He spun her into his arms and did a hip grind at the same time every other man participating in the dance did. Loud hoots drowned out the music.

Hands latched around Wren's waist, he rocked his hips into hers suggestively before dropping to a half-split.

Eyes wide with shock, she cupped her palms over her mouth. When he popped to his feet again, he grabbed her and gave her a twirl. Her squeal filled his ears, infectious enough to get his blood pounding.

The heavy thump of boots and drums hit his system. He spun Wren out again. This time she nearly toppled over, but he caught her and anchored her to his side. Holding her gaze, he started to move his feet, slowly at first, showing her the step.

She stumbled through a few imitations before she got it. Only then did he increase the speed. As she caught on, the music changed, but the dancers continued the steps for several more bars.

Jennings spun her out and then in. Her curves pressed against his body, and he ground his hips again.

"Woooo! Lucky woman!" a lady dancing near them cheered.

Wren's pretty face was lit with such happiness that it felt like a warm, cozy fire in his soul. Seeing the pink flush in her cheeks and the sparkle in her eyes drove him to put them there every single day.

Though she couldn't catch on to more than a few of the steps, she tried. Finally, she stood back, hand extended for him to do the honors for them both, and watched him finish out the dance.

The band switched gears, slowing things down so everyone could catch their breath. With his hand on Wren's ass, he brought her into his arms. They began to sway to the ballad about love and the girl next door.

He tucked her head under his chin. Her ear was pressed to his chest. "Your heart isn't even beating fast after all that."

He smiled down at her. "Lots of practice."

"You have a lot of talents I never would have guessed at."

"Not surprised. After all, your first impression of me was at the church."

Head tipped back, she studied his eyes. "I know you better now."

His lips quirked. "You did well keeping up with the dance."

At that, she tossed her head on a laugh. The sultry line of her throat invited his lips, and he couldn't help but lower his mouth to her pulse. She sucked in a sharp breath, fingers digging into the muscle of his shoulders.

Tracing the curve of her throat up to her ear, he drank in her delicious scent. "This dress..." He ran his hand over her rounded ass again. "It makes me want to find a dark corner."

Her breath hitched. "And do what?"

He nipped at her earlobe. "Yank it up. Tear off your panties and sink inside your tight pussy."

She sucked in a gasp. "This hat..."

He pierced her in his gaze. "You like it?"

160

"It's hot as hell."

They shared a knowing look that had his already hard cock stiffening to forged steel. "I think I've had enough of this birthday party."

* * * * *

The door of the rental that Jennings shared with Julius slammed shut, and he whirled Wren around. Her palms hit the wall and she barely dragged air into her lungs before his mouth landed on her neck and she forgot how to breathe again.

He sucked on her neck. Her nipples squeezed into sharp points. Liquid heat pooled low in her core.

"Are you going to..." she panted, "make good on your promise?"

"Mmhmm."

Back at the restaurant, his dirty talk about pulling up her dress and yanking off her panties had stolen her sanity. She barely recalled leaving the dance floor or saying hasty goodbyes to the Sentry team. When he put her into the car that Julius and Avalynn arrived in, she'd paused.

"What about your bike?"

"Can you ride in that dress?"

She glanced down at herself. He was right. The sheath dress was so fitted to her hips and thighs that she'd never be able to straddle it.

Now, Jennings eased his hand over her ass and lower, fingertips grazing her inner thigh. She cried out, and he coaxed her to widen her stance. When he trailed his fingers under the leg of her panties, her breath caught in her throat once again.

With his mouth at her ear, he breached her panties — and oh god, he stroked the wet folds of her pussy.

Need gripped her insides. She curled her fingers into the wall as though holding on tighter would stop the thunderous passion between them. This man ruled her body. He freakin' owned it with a single dark look.

He slipped his callused finger over her slick seam. A gasp never left her lips before he plunged his finger inside her. Her walls stretched. He burrowed deeper. With his big body pinning her to the wall, he shoved his finger in farther.

She rose onto the toes of the high heels that Lark finished off her outfit with. "Jennings!"

"Tell me what you want, baby." He withdrew his finger millimeter by millimeter, so slow that her walls began to clench and quiver.

"I want...two! Fingers!"

He fed a growl into her ear and thrust a second finger inside her. A tremor racked her. Need built and spread out like a fog around a mountain peak. She couldn't see the pinnacle but knew it was close. Just a little higher.

"Deeper!"

He jerked his hand, and her pussy flooded with juices. The throb in her core couldn't be stopped. Hell, it started back on that dance floor with the first grind of Jennings's hips. A hot guy who could dance was doubly sexy and rare as hell. If she were the type of woman who actually went out dancing—

Wait—she *was* that woman. Because of Jennings, her small life had begun to expand. She loved the company of her new friends, and more than once the sound of her own laugh had stunned her.

The rasp of her pleasure filled her ears now. Heart bursting with passion, she rocked her hips back into each plunge of her lover's fingers.

"That's it, baby. Come for me. Come all over my fingers—soak them. Then I'm going to suck your pussy clean and make you come again right before I take you."

The dirty words crashed into her mind and sent her over the edge.

Her pussy clamped on the fingers that he thrust hard and fast, lifting her higher onto tiptoe. When he reached around her body and pinched her nipple, she spun out of control.

The spiral of ecstasy whirled on and on and on. When she felt the wall at her back and Jennings's hot breath wash over her still-throbbing pussy, she realized he'd moved her to make good on the second part of his promise to lick her clean.

The first lap was an electric shock to her body. She ripped her hand off the wall and raked her fingers through his thick hair. When she tugged, bringing his lips and tongue deep into her wet folds, they shared a groan.

He licked. His tongue worked around and around her clit until it was stiff and straining.

She shook apart again, harder, her mouth open wide on a silent scream.

Hooking his finger into her throbbing channel again, he took her to a plane of bliss she floated on for so long that she didn't realize that he'd stripped her and she was kneeling before him until she looked up into his hooded eyes.

He fisted his cock at the base, the stiff length red with need. As he brought the mushroomed tip to her lips, she eagerly opened to take him.

The taste of lust and man exploded her tastebuds. Closing her lips around his veined shaft, she sucked him in. He sidled forward, thighs hard.

"God, love. Your mouth..." He ended the gritty words on a gulp.

Knowing that he loved what she was doing to him urged her to give back to her amazing partner with even more enthusiasm.

She sucked him deep into her throat and flicked her eyes up to see his reaction. Their gazes held. His blazed with so much tenderness.

Unable to look away, she sucked him deeper and was rewarded with a primal moan. His cock stiffened and angled deeper toward the back of her throat. She withdrew and never got to take him deep again because he hooked her under the arms and turned to the bed.

She threw her arms around his chiseled body, pulling him down on top of her. With her legs spread wide, there was no barrier between his cock and her pussy.

"Don't stop for a condom. I'm on the pill. I want you, Jennings!"

Something dark moved in the depth of his eyes. "There's no turning back if I take you this way. Do you understand me, love?"

The harsh tone of his voice sent her heart tumbling like a boulder down a steep hill. It never hit the bottom though—it felt as if it took off soaring instead.

His body seemed to strain with an internal battle. His cock head poised at her pussy, but he didn't claim her. "I sink my cock into you—with nothing between us—you're mine."

His for now. Jennings was fling material. She was okay with that.

But was he really changing? For her?

Chapter Thirteen

Bucking her hips upward, she urged him to claim her.

Could he even stop himself from doing exactly that?

All of a sudden, he saw a flash in his mind of life as it could be with Wren. Every man he knew had blazed the path for him. His grandfather. His own father, who doted on his momma. Jennings now saw why his old man got that soft look in his eyes whenever he chuckled over something he and Jennings's momma argued over.

Judd, Jace and Jaren, three of his brothers on the WEST Protection team, had fallen for amazing women. And Julius was now a husband and would soon be a father.

The last of his resistance crumbled. Jennings stared into Wren's beautiful eyes...and filled her with one thrust.

Scorching heat blasted through him. Her walls hugging him with nothing at all separating them felt amazing...but it was nothing compared to what was going on in his heart.

Swinging his hips forward, he pushed all the love he felt inside her. Their lips fused, their tongues tangling. Small moans escaped her, and he devoured them off her lips. The dark need pounding through his groin warned that he was close, but now that he was buried in the woman he loved, he wasn't about to lose control so soon.

He gritted his teeth and pounded her into the bed. The springs of the mattress bounced. Wren's throaty noises filled the room. The taste of her pussy lingered on his tongue, making his balls even heavier with the need to blow.

With his senses on overdrive came the sharp knowledge that he would kill any man who dared to lay a finger on this woman. All the dark alleys of his life, the things he'd done as a bodyguard and for Sentry, converged to this one singular point.

She whimpered. "Jennings! I'm...so...close!"

He captured her mouth, thrust his tongue inside and lost his grip in one stroke.

Hips jerking in the rhythm of mind-blowing release, he took her over the edge with him.

Jets of cum pulsed into her. The deep thrill of knowing that he was filling her with his cum made his orgasm all the more intense. He fucked her over and over until her roughened cries silenced and he collapsed on top of her.

The gentle sweep of her hand over his spine brought his brain cells back from the ether where they'd scattered the minute she did that thing with her tongue on his cock.

He drew away only enough to meet her gaze. The feel of her beneath him was too precious to let go of yet. "You are so beautiful."

The gentle smile tilting her lips felt like a tug on his heart. She twisted her lips into his shoulder and kissed it.

Leaning in, he brushed his mouth across her temple before rolling off. Even though he didn't want to be one of those guys who talked after sex, practically asking for verification that they'd given a great performance, he needed to know.

"What made you do it?"

She locked gazes with him. "Do what?"

"Ask me to skip the condom."

The flush in her cheeks deepened to a dark rose. "It was probably you moving on that dance floor."

Caught off guard by her answer, he barked a laugh. "We can head back right now if it means I get to turn you on again. The restaurant's still open."

She threw her arm around him and held on tight. "I'm not up for embarrassing myself any further today."

He stroked a lock of warm brown hair off her face. "You were great."

"Now you're lying to me."

They shared a quiet laugh. Then he sobered. "The team loves you."

She blinked. "How do you know that?"

"I know them. They're like my own brothers. Their wives are my sisters. We're like a big family. Now they're your family too."

She turned her stare up to the ceiling, her smile vanishing and a tiny pucker appearing between her brows. "My brother is all I have."

"Not anymore, love."

She stared at him. "I'm not sure what to think of all this. This isn't any world I know or understand."

"What do you mean?" He felt the hum of tension brewing just under her silky flesh and locked a hand on her hip to hold her there with him.

"These are your people, not mine."

"You're not alone now."

"The ladies are fantastic, but they were just being nice to me."

He gaped at her. "You really don't know how special you are, do you?"

"I'm nothing special, Jennings. I'm a washed-up med student stuck in a dead-end job. I hope that my brother cleans up, but I know the statistics. It can take several stays in rehab to finally get clean. I have no delusions about my brother, and when this is all over, I'm going to leave town. Start over."

Her words stung, each syllable a slash to his flesh. Blood filled in those cuts.

When he looked at her again, he shook his head. "If you leave town, I'm coming with you."

Alarm suffused her gaze. "What? No. You belong here with your team and your...f-found...f-family." The tremor in her voice made him grip her tighter, but she rolled out of bed and strode to the bathroom before he could stop her.

Flopping onto his back, he slung his arm over his eyes. Damn. Five minutes earlier, he decided to embrace this relationship, and he'd already messed up. Thing was, he wasn't even sure what he'd said to upset her.

A few minutes later, she emerged from the bathroom. She crossed the room and scooped her clothes off the floor. "I need to return to Spring Valley. I have work."

He sat up and reached for her, but she took a step out of reach of even his long arms. Unsure what to do, he scrubbed his palms over his face.

"All right. I'll drive you back...but we have to stay at the club. You know that, right?"

A heavy heartbeat ticked by before she nodded in agreement.

The hopelessness bowing her slender shoulders damn near broke his heart. He hated whatever this battle going on inside her was, but he hated even more that she was losing it.

Well, Jennings wasn't going to give up on Wren. What she didn't know was that he was a persistent motherfucker, and he *always* got what he wanted.

* * * * *

Walking into the nursing home brought on an instant reminder of what happened on her last shift with the patient's grandson. In the end, she'd sent him running, but that didn't mean the next shift hadn't allowed him back into the room and broken the rules by leaving up the administration of pills to a family member.

She also hadn't slept. The party in the Disciples clubhouse ended with a bunch of guys running outside and shooting guns into the air for hours. Every shot had her teeth gritting and a small scream trapped behind her teeth. In the early hours before daylight, she'd fallen into a fitful sleep and woken to Jennings shaking her.

She slogged through the hallways on her rounds, checking in on the people in the memory care wing. Usually these patients suffered from dementia or Alzheimer's and some had forgotten how to put on their clothes or feed themselves. Often her job went beyond the physical, though, and she spent a lot of time just talking to them and hearing what stories they remembered far better than what they had for breakfast only an hour before.

171

As she walked through the hallway to the nurse's station, Janine was headed the opposite direction. A smile broke over her face, and she bounced up to Wren.

"Hey, girl! We've been on opposing shifts the past couple days. I never got the scoop on that guy you're seeing!" She leaned in to whisper, "Is he bad in bed yet?"

Everything that happened overnight, and especially her letting Jennings take her so intimately had her in a tailspin, but Janine's question threw her off. She giggled.

"I'm not one to kiss and tell." She skirted around her friend and took off walking.

Janine followed her. "C'mon now. You can't leave a girl hanging. I saw him waiting for you outside on a motorcycle. It's not every day that a man *that hot* walks into your world. The least you can do is let me live vicariously!"

Again, Wren laughed. "He's fine, and yes, I *can* leave you hanging. I'm not giving you more particulars about my sex life."

She folded her arms and shot Wren a smug look. "That means he's great. I knew it."

If Wren denied it, then Janine would only have more ammunition to fire at her and more questions that she didn't want to answer.

Her brain was already packed with worries when it came to Jennings. Being out with him and his team had felt far too much like a family gathering. Sharing food and watching Quaide blow out the candles on his birthday cake got to her. How long since she had experienced anything so normal as a birthday celebration?

She'd stopped caring about her own birthdays after her parents died, and Danny's came and went without any ways to mark the passing of time. Last year, she hadn't heard from him at all and the only way she acknowledged his special day was by walking by a bakery and pausing to stare in the front window at a display of beautiful cupcakes. She'd whispered "happy birthday" to her brother, wherever he was, and continued on.

Compared to the fantastic food and company of Quaide's party, that seemed even sadder now. Add in dancing with the man who wasn't just a fantastic lover but treated her to other pleasures of life, and she didn't know what to do with all these emotions tying her up in knots.

It would be so easy to let him sweep her away like Prince Charming. But it wasn't reality.

A shout from the end of the hall tore her from her deep thoughts. She and Janine exchanged a glance and took off running. One of the security guards joined them just as they reached Mr. Craig's room.

At first, she didn't see anybody in the room. The bed was empty, the sheets balled up at the bottom.

Wren ran inside and looked in the bathroom. Then she spun around and spotted Mr. Craig curled up in the corner of the room, his arms thrown over his head as if hunkering down from an incoming missile.

"Get his sedative!" she called to Janine.

The orderly took a step toward the man, and he let out a bellow. "Keep away from me!"

Wren sliced a hand through the air. "Stay back. Let me talk to him. He's done this before. He believes he's in the war."

"Everybody get away from me!" He started shoving at invisible enemies.

Seconds later, Janine returned with a syringe of medication to calm Mr. Craig's nerves. Wren eyed her coworker.

"I'll talk to him, distract him. I'll try to coax him back to bed. If that doesn't work, you move around behind and give him the injection."

Janine bobbed her head in agreement.

"Mr. Craig, how are you today? It looks like you might be having some trouble."

His wild eyes rolled side to side, anywhere but on her. He took a swing at one of the invisible people he thought were attacking him.

"I hate everyone! They all need to leave me alone."

"I think everyone feels that way sometimes." Her statement gave him pause.

His stare shifted to her. "What do you know about anything? You're young. You have your whole life ahead of you. I'm stuck in here with all these people yelling at me!"

She took a step closer to him and then another. "That's true, Mr. Craig. But that doesn't mean I don't have troubles too. Let me help you. Is your back giving you pain again? I can give you some medication to give you some relief."

"You can leave me alone too," he muttered.

This wouldn't be easy. She continued trying to talk him back to bed for ten more minutes. Finally, she gave Janine a look, and she darted around Mr. Craig and delivered the injection in one quick jab.

He silenced at once. Then he slumped over.

"Help me get him in bed," Wren ordered the guard. Together, the three of them lifted the man and carefully laid him in bed. She made sure to put the side rails up and secure him to the frame with soft restraints.

Only then did she release the breath she'd been holding. She dragged a hand over her face, trying to collect herself. Things like this didn't happen every day, but they were upsetting for everyone involved. Seeing the distress on Mr. Craig's face wasn't easy to shake off.

Janine knew this as well. She moved to Wren and rested her arm over her shoulders. "Come on. Let's take a short break. We'll walk around the garden and look at the flowers they just planted."

175

She nodded and moved off with Janine while the guard remained in front of Mr. Craig's door to watch over him.

On the way outside, they stopped to talk to the head nurse and fill her in on the incident. When they made their escape into the small private garden where families and patients often congregated for visits, Wren walked straight to a bench and plopped down.

Janine came to sit next to her.

Long minutes passed while neither of them spoke. Birds chirped and somewhere in a distant part of town, a lawnmower hummed. So normal. But Wren's life felt far from it.

"When are you going to make a break for it, Wren?"

Startled, she looked up at Janine. "What are you talking about?"

"You were in medical school before coming here. When are you going back?"

She stared into space for a long heartbeat. "Maybe never."

Janine shook her head. "That would be such a shame."

"It's too difficult now. I'm too old. Adulting caught up with me."

"That shouldn't keep you from your dreams."

She gazed at her friend, seeing that Janine cared about her more than just as a coworker. She had Wren's best interests at heart.

"Life's too short to be stuck here, Wren. I don't know all of your story, but I know you've had it hard. That's an even better reason to keep working toward your goal to become a doctor."

She swallowed the lump of salt in her throat. "Maybe you're right."

"Oh, I am."

They looked at each other and broke out laughing at the confident way Janine said that.

When they finished having a chuckle—and dispelling a good measure of stress from what just happened with Mr. Craig—Wren touched her friend's forearm. "Thank you for being such a good friend. I needed it."

Janine got to her feet. "I bet if you look around, you have quite a few people who care about you a lot."

Long after she walked away, Wren continued to sit there, thinking that her friend might be right.

Chapter Fourteen

"Hey, hey! It's Jay!" Mack clapped Jennings on the back hard enough to bruise before he made it a step into the club.

Turning to the guy, he gave him a chin lift in greeting and shrugged off the blow to the back he'd taken from the huge guy. Holding out his fist, he bumped knuckles with Mack.

"Hey, Jay." The sultry blonde with dark eye makeup wrapped herself around Mack, her long fingernails red against the black leather he wore.

"What's been going on around here?" He swept his gaze around the room. The usual number of Disciples were hanging out.

Mack jabbed a thick finger at the back of the room. "Mean game of pool happening. Jake the Snake is getting his snake charmed over in the corner."

Jennings skimmed a look over the guy sitting on the couch, his cock buried in the throat of a fake redhead. That guy got more oral in one week than most men received in their lives.

Disgusted, he twisted away. His stare landed on something much, much worse.

Fuck. It was Bones. The guy who took Jennings along on that drug run.

He'd also been in the church. He was one of the few who knew that Jennings was there at the same time that Viper went missing.

He was staring back at Jennings.

In a blink he sized up the situation. Bones wasn't the smartest, but he couldn't be clueless or the club wouldn't hold him in such high esteem and entrust him with their drug trade. That meant that Bones was capable of putting two and two together and coming to the conclusion that Jennings had something to do with Viper's disappearance.

Fuck.

He'd play it cool and bide his time. But if anything came up, he wouldn't hesitate to act.

At least Wren was at work. Bones couldn't see her and make speculations.

Mack caught his attention again. "Cole needs to talk to you."

He nodded. "Thanks, man." He smacked Mack on the back equally as hard as he had. He didn't stick around to watch his reaction but made his way across the room toward Cole.

Cole saw him and flicked his fingers for him to follow him. The room in the back was one Jennings had only been in a handful of times—the first time when they patched him in.

As they walked in, he caught the scent of marijuana and cigars.

Cole turned to him. "I need you to do something for the club."

Adrenaline trickled into Jennings's system.

This was it. They were sending him on another drug run. He'd gather the rest of the information they needed to make the sting and bring down the Disciples.

"Sure. Anything you need, Cole."

He reached two fingers into the leather pocket of his cut and extracted a slip of paper.

Jennings took it with a cocked brow. "This important, boss?"

"Yeah. There's a big party tonight for the prez. We need supplies."

Sliding his gaze from Cole, he glanced at the paper he held. He expected an address where he would be picking up the drugs himself. Or how the duffel bags got into the hands of the dealers. Or where the takeout bags at Shadowlands went after people picked them up.

If he got the last missing pieces of the puzzle, he could get out of the club and take Wren with him.

He skimmed the paper.

Cases of Beer
Vodka

Barbecue from Skinny D's
Cake

He looked up. "You want me to make a run to the grocery store?"

"Yeah. Use the club vehicle. Take care of this for us, would you? It would mean a lot to the prez knowing that you had a hand in his party. He likes to put trust in his new patches."

Jennings's veins filled with red-hot anger. The molten flow scorched him.

"Any questions?" Cole eyed him.

"Nope. Easy run." He held up the paper that he pinched hard enough to crush into pulp. "Won't take me long."

Without another word, Cole nodded to him. Jennings walked out. On the way through the club, he glanced to where Bones had been standing. They locked gazes once more.

The hair on his nape prickled.

Game on.

He strode out, aware of footsteps behind him. When he pushed out the door, he braced himself for what came next.

Tossing a glance over his shoulder, he strode in the opposite direction of the car he was supposed to use. In a fast clip, he rounded the corner of the building.

When Bones cleared the corner, Jennings hooked his arm around his neck and threw him to the ground. Bones scrabbled, but Jennings was bigger and stronger.

Using his body weight, he braced his forearm over his throat while fishing in his pocket. He wasn't searching for the goddamn shopping list—he whipped out a zip-tie and in a swift move, shoved him face down and bound his hands behind his back.

Bones inflated his lungs to let out a bellow, but Jennings cut that off. He clamped his hand on the guy's neck, compressing the pressure point and knocking him out. His adversary went boneless.

Looking around to make sure no one witnessed what he'd done, he gained his feet and hefted Bones over his shoulder. At the corner, he paused to glance at the parking lot. Seeing that no one was out there, he rushed to the car. The cameras he could deal with by hacking the system through his phone. He dumped Bones on the ground out of sight.

He whipped open the front door and pushed the button to pop the trunk. In seconds, he had Bones loaded in and a nice length of duct tape over his mouth.

After he jumped behind the wheel, he issued a low growl. Goddammit. Stuffing a man in the trunk was *not* part of the plan. He needed to get rid of him, but he needed to pick up those damn supplies quickly to stay in good graces with the Disciples. Playing this game was getting old, though. He wanted out and Wren safe.

He zoomed through traffic, blew a couple red lights and arrived at the store in minutes. The guy in the trunk wouldn't rouse for a while longer, so he was confident that he wouldn't wake up and pound on the trunk to alert someone he was inside.

He took a minute to wipe the footage from the club cameras that surveilled the parking lot and then climbed out.

In the store, Jennings grabbed a shopping cart, mentally gnashing his teeth at the idea of buying food and alcohol for those fuckers at the club. He had more pressing matters to deal with.

He rushed through the aisles, loading the cart with cases of beer. He'd have to swing by the liquor store for vodka, which would give him more time to call Lexis and unload Bones on him.

Glancing at the list, he whipped around the corner and slammed his cart right into another customer's.

"Damn, sorry—" He broke off as he locked stares with a very familiar set of eyes.

"What the fuck are you doing here?" he hissed at Julius. Fury hit him like a wave. "Don't answer that— you're checking up on me. You never had any goddamn faith in my ability."

Julius had a few items in his cart that looked as random as his brother being in this store in a different town. He stepped closer to Jennings and lowered his voice. "I prefer to think of it as having your back. You've been distracted by a certain person."

He let out a warning growl. "I've never been more focused," he bit off. "I just handed you all those leads. And I've got my own back."

"Not distracted? The old Jennings would have noticed I was here ten minutes ago."

He inflated his lungs to bursting. His rage turned inward. *Dammit.* His brother wasn't wrong.

"I've got a lot on my mind."

"I knew I should have—"

He shoved his face an inch from Julius's. "If you finish that sentence, I swear to god we're gonna brawl right here. Don't you dare say you should have been undercover instead of me."

To his shock, Julius rocked back a step. Then another.

Now that he had some breathing room, he realized that his brother showing up here actually provided the help he needed.

He leaned close. "By the way, there's something in my trunk I need you to take care of for me."

Julius cocked a brow.

Wordlessly, Jennings finished the grocery shopping and paid for the purchases. Julius bought the random pistachios, olive oil and cleaning spray in his cart and trailed him to the car a minute later.

He popped the trunk and they stared down at Bones. His eyes were open and filled with fury.

Julius heaved a sigh. "Fuck."

* * * * *

Wren poised her fingertip over the contact on her phone for the rehab facility. Her heart throbbed in rhythmic bursts, fast or slow, based on what noises were around her.

The sound of two nurses talking just outside the break room door had her heart galloping until they moved away. Then it slowed a bit, allowing her to catch her breath.

Sentry warned her about calling her brother, but she really, really needed to hear his voice, for him to tell her that he was all right, and she'd made the right decisions for both of them.

She set her phone on the table next to the slice of pizza she'd pulled out of the employee fridge. For so long, stress had caused her stomach to cramp and made it difficult to eat at times just like this.

I don't have to call. I shouldn't call. He's okay where he is and doesn't need to hear from me.

She needed the connection with someone who knew her. Someone who cared.

Jennings's rough and rugged features loomed in her mind. If he saw her now, he'd pull her into his lap and make her feel safe. He'd brush his lips across her brow.

185

And she'd hang on tight to him, because Jennings had become her rock.

She really needed to stop thinking about that man. When this was all over, she could return to her dull life of work and loneliness. He would— Well, who knew what Jennings would do after he walked away from her.

She issued a slow sigh and shut off her phone. The black screen gave her a wakeup call about her life. She truly was in this alone. Once her brother got out, he might remain sober, but that didn't mean he'd be there for her. She had to face reality.

She wouldn't miss the club at all. But the Sentry team had been great to her. And Jennings...

She pushed out another sigh. The rumble of voices had her glancing at the time. Damn, she'd wasted her entire break sitting here trying to decide whether or not to call Danny. Now she didn't even have time to eat.

She got up and tossed the food in the trash. Then she scooped up her phone and swung toward the door.

A voice reached her. Low. Distinct. It had a soothing note right now, as if the speaker were pacifying somebody. But she only remembered the anger echoing from the speakerphone in that church.

Sucking in a sharp breath, she inched to the doorway. The man was down the hall and to the right. The singsong rise and dip of his tone sounded different from the bellowing he was capable of.

She gripped her phone. Calling Jennings would bring him running—and perhaps the entire Sentry team with him. But they might miss the man.

After listening a minute longer, she realized his voice was fading away. He was moving down the corridor.

She had one chance.

Darting out of the break room, she cast a look around for the man. Just up ahead, past the nurse's station. He paused to say goodbye to the nurses sitting there doing patient charts.

Wren hung back, giving him time to finish and go on his way.

When he began walking toward the exit, her heart leaped in her chest again. As it somersaulted over and over, she swiped her fear away and trailed the man outside.

He crossed the parking lot to a white car with a luxury emblem.

As he slid behind the wheel, she got into position to watch him drive out of the lot.

Her phone! Covertly, she held her phone in a way that he wouldn't see where it was aimed from this distance. She snapped a photo of his license plate just as he drove away from the nursing home.

With shaking hands, she lifted her phone and stared at the photo. Expanding it, she was able to pick out every letter and number of the license plate, as well as a sticker in the back window with the name of the church she recognized him from.

A tiny gasp escaped her, and she stabbed a button for another contact. When Jennings's voice filled her ear, she issued a cry of relief.

"Are you okay?" His voice rumbled with all that yummy alpha goodness of the protector she knew him to be. Her stomach pooled with lust.

Remembering why she called him in the first place, she blurted, "I have a plate!"

Background noises of chatter and things banging around alerted her that he was not alone and probably unable to take this call.

"You're at the club."

"Yes." The clipped syllable made her think of how his jaw clenched.

"You can't speak freely."

"Not right this second. I'll come get you. Give me—"

"No," she broke in. "I'll call someone else. Clay!" The solution seemed like the right course of action. Lark had programmed all their numbers into Wren's phone while she insisted that Wren apply lipstick and mascara in the back of the SUV.

"Wait—"

Something smashed in the background, and wild laughter exploded.

She quickly ended the call and dialed Clay. It went to voicemail, but what was she going to say in a message? She could call the cops, give them the plate and... What? Tell them that she had been with a drug dealer in the back of a church? Then a guy from the FBI task force came in and killed the drug dealer who took her as compensation because her brother witnessed a murder and crossed him?

The story was too big for her to even begin to retell.

The back of the nursing home didn't have a pretty garden to enjoy while she struggled with such a heavy dilemma. A couple dumpsters and some HVAC units were lined up along a wall that looked as drab and dreary as it was inside some days.

When the wind blew a lock of hair into her eye, she remembered she actually needed to get back to work. She'd just have to wait until she was alone with Jennings to share the photo of the license plate with him.

She turned to the door but stopped short when her phone buzzed with a call.

She jerked it to her ear. "Yes?"

"Wren? It's Lark. Is everything okay? I saw you called Clay."

"Thank goodness! I got something. A picture."

"Okay," she said slowly. "Of what?"

Afraid some landscaper might be lurking around outside to overhear, she stole a peek at her surroundings before telling Lark about hearing the voice from the church and how she'd followed him outside and snapped a picture of his license plate.

"Send it to me." Lark's take-charge tone filled her with relief. Having backup was good—she'd been running this ship of life as the captain *and* crew for far too long. She was tired…and confused by everything happening right now.

As Lark instructed, she shot the photo off to Clay's phone.

"Good—now delete everything. Your call history, the photo and that text."

"I'm doing it now." She quickly performed the tasks. "I have to go."

"Okay. You did a great thing. Are you sure you want to go back to med school?"

The question caught her by surprise.

"Why are you asking?"

"Because you're really good at this line of work, and you *are* a bird name."

A laugh bubbled up, throwing her even more off course. "Now I think you're reaching, Lark."

She giggled. "Just trying to show you that you really belong with us."

Her words sank in.

Shaking her head, she said, "I think you're wrong, Lark. I don't belong. You guys are all in relationships. And Jennings…he's only a fling."

The scuff of a boot on the ground made Wren whirl. A set of dark eyes pinned her in place.

With a gulp, she lowered the phone from her ear and quickly ended the call.

He took a step closer to her. She backed up.

Hooking out a long arm, Jennings snagged her around the middle and yanked her *flush* against him. Every hard inch of his body made her own thrum. The glare he settled on her was offset by the determined way he leaned in.

"Only a fling, Wren?"

Her heart threatened to pound out of her chest. Unable to find any words, she simply attempted a nod.

He kissed her hard, tongue thrusting deep in her mouth and stealing a cry from her throat. She latched on to his shoulders, yanking him down for more and more.

Too soon, he tore from the kiss. Chest heaving, he stared at her mouth as if she were a decadent—but naughty—treat.

She fought to rearrange her scrambled brain cells, to remember what they were discussing.

Oh. That was right. What they had was just a fling.

He stroked his thumb over the corner of her mouth, and her nipples peaked. "This is not a fling, Wren. This"—he tugged her even tighter against his

191

bulging erection—"is real. Every word, every look...every *inch*."

Her mouth dried out.

"Maybe I'm..." Her tongue seemed glued to the roof of her mouth. She tried again. "Maybe I'm wrong."

His eyes narrowed on her. "You know what you *are*, baby?"

She shook her head, dizzy from the dark waves of desire crashing over her.

"You." He nipped her bottom lip.

"Are." He ground his hips against hers and pinched her straining nipple.

"Mine."

Chapter Fifteen

Half the club was hungover from the president's party. The other half was still passed out on sofas and in various corners.

Jennings wrinkled his nose at the sour smell of vomit.

He had avoided drinking too much, but the guys made it difficult to turn down shots. In the end, he'd relied on his size and alcohol tolerance to make sure he got Wren safely to their bed.

And still had plenty of stamina to give her two writhing, gasping orgasms.

A hand came down on his shoulder, jerking him from his reverie of hooking Wren's ankles over his shoulders and pounding her into the mattress.

When he took her to work, they slipped out the back door and luckily avoided the aftereffects of the all-nighter.

With a sigh, he walked behind the bar, grabbed the trash can and started filling it with empty bottles. The beer had run out within the first two hours of the festivities, and then everyone turned to the heavier stuff.

He dropped a couple bottles into the can. The *clank* roused a man lying face down on the sofa with his head pillowed on a woman's bare thigh.

"Huh? What's going on?" the guy mumbled.

Jennings patted him on the shoulder. "Just the cleanup crew." He looked closer at the guy.

Damn, it was Matthews. And the woman was Tilly. Well, he must be feeling better after being shot and the ordeal of being fixed up in the clubhouse.

He'd relay the information to Wren that her patient had not only survived but lived through a drunken orgy in the prez's honor.

After he'd cleared off about half the tables, someone called his name.

Jennings looked up to see Cole standing in the doorway.

"Come with me." He crooked a finger.

He set down the can and followed, stepping over a guy's legs. What the hell did Cole want from him now? If he was just sending him for more food and booze, Julius would never let him live it down, even though he wasn't at fault for the slow grind of club crimes.

He wondered what the hell Julius did with Bones, but he didn't have time to call and ask now.

When Jennings walked into the room, his gaze fell on the half-dozen Disciples seated at the long table.

His senses tripped. Something was going down. Either he was outed and they were going to jump him, or he was finally big-time.

"Take a seat, Jay." Cole waved at the empty chairs.

He slid one out, scraping the feet on the floor, and sank into it.

A glance at the men showed how serious the situation was. And most of the guys had clear eyes, indicating they hadn't drunk as much as the others.

"Down to business." Cole took up his seat near the head of the table, but the place of honor was reserved for their president, who was not present. At this point in his illustrious career as the leader of the huge gang, he didn't need to do the dirty work himself.

Cole looked around the table. "Here's the plan. You and you," he pointed to two members, "take the van."

"Ten passenger, boss?"

"Yeah. We need the room."

Jennings's ears perked up, and the video film of his brain began to roll, recording every detail.

He played it cool, listening to the schedule of events. Take the van south, and leave after this meeting.

Cole passed out more jobs to the others, leaving only Jennings to question whether or not he was here to receive a duty or if he'd be handed a grocery list.

At last, Cole fixed Jennings in his gaze. "You and I will be flying to El Paso."

He tried not to reveal any outward reaction, just waited for more information.

"We board the flight around three in the morning. It gives the guys who are driving enough of a jump. By the time we get to El Paso and do what we need to do, they'll have the vans at the ready."

He was strangely calm. Prepared for anything. Capable of handling every detail.

"Got it, boss. Any instruction on what to do in the meantime?"

"Yeah, quit being such an overachiever, Jay. Leave the cleanup to the whores." His words earned a ripple of laughter around the table.

Before he could respond to that order, everyone shoved away from the table and sauntered out.

He started to get up too, but Cole waved him back down. Jennings settled his arms on the table, leaning forward slightly. "Yeah, boss?"

"You could pick up some food at the bar this evening before we go."

He bobbed his head. "No problems. Any requests?"

"Just call and tell them our usual order. That should cover it."

"Order" could mean a hell of a lot of things.

"Got it. I'll hit the bar and be ready for the flight."

Cole didn't say more, so Jennings took that as a sign of dismissal.

As he walked out, a growl began in his chest. Something big was going down—he could feel it. And everything in him told him to get Wren out. Now.

She couldn't vanish. But maybe they could fabricate a story about her going to visit her sister or a sick grandparent. Since his jerk brother couldn't stay out of Jennings's op, he was most likely hanging around Spring Valley. It would be no trouble for him to pick up Wren from work and take her to a safehouse.

But that meant being away from her, and Jennings's jaw clenched at the very thought.

What he told her—that she was his—was true to the core of his soul. In their short time, he felt as if a bond had been forged so strong, so indestructible, that he couldn't even fathom leaving her, even with a man he trusted as much as he did his own brother.

In a few hours, he'd be on a plane to El Paso. Wren couldn't go unprotected within the walls of the club, and she definitely wasn't returning to that dump she called her apartment. In his line of work, he knew *far* too much about the happenings in that neighborhood.

Damn. He didn't have a choice. He had to call in his team.

197

Outside, a few guys were hanging around, checking out each other's bikes. Not unusual in the club. One man lay on the ground, a wrench in hand, adjusting what looked like the carburetor.

As Jennings passed them, he lifted his chin in acknowledgement before he reached his own bike. The helmet dangling from the handlebar was his own. Too large for Wren, yet she looked so damn adorable in it. Now he couldn't even look at the protective headgear without seeing her wearing it.

He was racing against the clock. Wren was in danger just because of her association with him.

Fuck, what was he thinking? He'd killed a man. Out of self-defense, sure, but dumping the body of a drug dealer that worked closely with the Disciples was asking to end up in a body bag himself.

There was also the matter of Bones. Without question, Sentry had the man in FBI custody. But he'd been seen leaving the club right after Jennings.

He swung his leg over his bike. The engine rolled over, purring like the wild animal he'd personally built it to be with his own two hands. At one time, he would have said that bike was the only thing he needed in his life. That happiness was the open road and the freedom of speed.

Now he missed the feel of his woman wrapped around him and knowing that when they stopped, he'd have her in his arms.

He had to get her to safety.

When he pulled off the highway into a roadside barbecue joint, he pulled out his phone and called Lexis.

"I've got something," he told his boss.

"I'm listening."

"I'm not sure what's going down, but I'm headed to El Paso with the VP."

"Shit. When?"

"Tonight. By jet."

"I'll have Lark look up the air marshall on that flight and make sure he's got your six."

"I could use it. But I don't expect any issues on the flight. Hell, I don't even know if it's a traditional flight. There's a van of guys meeting us upon arrival. Not sure what the plan really is, but it's big."

"We'll be listening for chatter."

"I need a favor," he blurted.

Lexis was silent for a heartbeat. Then he said, "Is it Wren?"

"Yeah. She's at work. I'm going to pick her up, put in an appearance at the bar." He hadn't fully constructed a plan but now it rolled off his tongue as if it'd been in the back of his head all this time.

"Drop us a pin to a rendezvous point and we'll get her out safe."

Emotion clogged his throat. "You'll need to watch out for—"

"We got you," Lexis cut off his words.

199

He scrubbed a hand over his face. "I don't like this."

"I understand. But let us do this for you—for the team."

"The team?"

"Lark seems to think that Wren belongs with Sentry."

That lump in his throat doubled in size. He pinched the bridge of his nose. "She might not be wrong. We can't fuck this up, Lexis."

"We won't. Keep us updated about where to pick her up, and we'll be there. Then you make goddamn sure you watch your back."

He couldn't fail. He had too much to lose, and it was more than the op at this point.

When he ended the call, he focused on the people coming and going from the barbecue joint. He didn't spot anyone who might report to the Disciples that he pulled off and talked on the phone, so he put his helmet back on and rolled out.

The loop around town to reach the nursing home didn't take long. His mind was deeply engrossed in what to tell Wren about the situation. And how much was too much. She was savvy, probably more street smart than a lot of people he'd met. But one look at her big eyes invited him to wrap himself around her like a shield.

* * * * *

200

Wren's nerves jangled. Ever since Jennings showed up at work and said those things to her, she had been aching to be with him again, to have his arms around her, pulling her close. His lips on hers.

She stood at the nurse's station, plugging information into the computer for the last patient she'd assisted. Every few words of her report, she glanced down at the clock in the corner of the screen.

Janine appeared at Wren's side. "Is it just me or is this the longest day ever?"

"It is," Wren agreed.

"All the days probably feel long to you. You can't wait to get back to that hot man of yours." She bumped her shoulder into Wren's playfully. "Damn, you're lucky."

Wren's fingers stilled on the keys. *Lucky.*

She'd never looked at her life from that perspective before. After all she had endured following their parents' deaths, she considered herself a survivor. So what if she didn't finish medical school? She had training for a decent job that was in high demand.

Though the reason why wasn't ideal, her dream of her brother getting into rehab had come true. Instead of being trapped with a drug dealer, Jennings swooped in like a hero and rescued her.

She'd found love.

And an *amazing* sex life.

"Three minutes till this day's over." She saved the reporting and closed the patient file. "I'm going to grab my purse and be ready to fly out the door. I'm not taking any chances at being stuck here longer."

Janine laughed. "Hurry! Enjoy your night." She sent her a wink.

Wren rushed to the employee area and grabbed her handbag. By the time she reached the front and set eyes on the big, tall man in black leather, her stomach was doing flips.

He twisted toward the door as soon as it opened. Dark eyes struck her, filling her with liquid heat.

She lengthened her strides. Jennings met her halfway. She tucked her purse over her shoulder to loop her arms around his neck. Going on tiptoe, she captured his mouth.

A deep growl rumbled in his chest. Angling his head, he deepened the caress but didn't claim her with the same level of heat he reserved for the bedroom. Instead, he brushed his mouth tenderly over hers once…twice.

They pulled apart. The corner of his lips quirked. "You missed me, huh?"

"Maybe I didn't get enough of you after that surprise visit."

The other corner of his mouth hitched up. Her breath caught in her chest. When Jennings smiled, the dark, dim parts of the world — and her existence — lit up with a warm golden glow.

"Ready to ride?"

She nodded, and he led her to the bike with a hand on her spine. Tingles swept through her and a knot tightened low in her belly.

They only drove a short distance before he took a turn that he never had before.

"Where are we going?" She raised her voice to be heard.

He didn't answer her, but seconds later they stopped. He cut the engine and pivoted his head to look back at her. "We need to talk."

That warmth in her veins turned to ice. "About what?"

"Things are happening. In two days, this will all be over, Wren."

"The op? Or..."

He twisted even more. "Were you going to say 'us?' Hell no, baby. If everything goes to plan, I'll be out of this op by the end of the week. I have to go out of town first. I made arrangements for you."

Her heart lurched. "What kind of arrangements?" Suddenly, she felt like a pet that needed care when the owner went on vacation.

"I need you to be seen with me. We'll go to the bar. Pick up food for the club. Then one of my teammates from Sentry will take you somewhere safe."

An entire iceberg sat in her stomach, deadly and spiked.

"You think I'm still in danger?"

"We both are. I can't take any more risks with you than I already have."

She curled her fingers around his bicep. "You've done so much for me, Jennings."

He didn't look convinced. She traced the line of his crinkled brow with the pad of her thumb. Then she dropped her forehead to his neck, breathing in the scent of leather and man.

"I never thought I'd have something like this with any man. Jennings, I—"

He cut across her. "Don't say it now, Wren."

She pinched her eyes shut. Pain stabbed through her. He didn't need to explain why he didn't want her admissions right now. Somehow, she understood that the timing wasn't right.

She'd take what she could get. Right this moment, she had her arms around the man she loved, and he cared about her enough to keep her safe.

When he started the engine again, she tightened her hold on him, imprinting the feel of his strong body in her mind as they took the turns. Minutes later, they parked in front of the Shadowlands.

With his arm slung around her shoulders, he made a show of entering the bar with her. Going from the bright evening sunshine to the dark wood-paneled walls made her blink to adjust her eyes. Jennings didn't seem to have the same trouble, though, and walked with confidence up to the bar.

There, he stopped and turned to her. "You hungry? What do you say about grabbing a couple burgers and fries for ourselves?"

"Yeah, babe. That sounds good," she simpered, hanging on him the way she'd seen the girls drape themselves on the Disciples in the club.

He patted her ass. "Want to grab us a place to sit and I'll order?"

"Sure thing." She wandered away from him, suddenly aware of a lot of eyes on her. And probably on Jennings too. His reason for sending her away was clear—he needed to exchange some information or speak to somebody.

Next to the table she chose sat an old jukebox. Distracted, she leaned over it and started reading the song titles.

A few feet away, she caught movement through one of the few windows in this place.

Her heart froze. Air trapped in her throat.

The car.

The one from the nursing home. The very same car that she'd snapped a photo of and sent to Lexis.

Slowly, she turned to glance at Jennings.

"That's her," someone from the next table hissed to his companion. "The nurse. His sister."

Heart thundering, she battled with the decision to stay or run. One thing she was certain of: she had to get to Jennings.

"Call him. Tell him she's here in the bar. The nurse sister is here. She was with the dead drug dealer."

She clenched her fingers on the glass of the jukebox. The titles blurred in her vision.

To rush out would only alert these men who were discussing her as if she weren't standing mere feet away after her.

But if they knew who she was, then they probably knew Jennings too.

"That biker was at the church too," the man said in a low rumble to his companion. "Tell him the biker is with the nurse. He killed the drug dealer."

Terror blasted through Wren. They *knew* Jennings killed Viper? If so, why had they waited for so long to find Jennings? A man of his size and confidence was far from invisible, especially in a town like this.

He'd told her this this op was ending. But how?

That car was outside. And in here, people knew them. Knew what they'd done.

When she cast him a look over her shoulder, he took one glance at her face and broke off the conversation he was having with the bartender. He started toward her.

She spun and rushed to his side, even more aware that every set of eyes in the bar pinned on them.

He clasped her hand hard enough to crack her bones and yanked her to the door. As soon as they cleared the entrance, he ordered, "Run!"

Fear clutching at her stomach, she shot forward with Jennings dragging her to his bike.

"Get on!" He jumped on in front her. She barely had her thighs locked around him and her arms around his middle before the bike roared to life and they made a break for the road.

Chapter Sixteen

Jennings thought his days of speed were over. But he never guessed that he'd be involved in a chase with the woman he loved on the back of his bike.

Just knowing that she was a target sent his instincts into overdrive. He punched the gas and hit a speed that would snap both their necks if he struck so much as a pebble.

He had no destination in mind—just get out of town, hide Wren.

He glanced down at the gas gauge and his stomach bottomed out. Hell, he probably left his balls half a mile back on the road when he felt the chug of the engine that told him the tank was on empty.

"Fuck!" His curse got snatched by the wind, and if Wren heard, she couldn't comment anyway over the road noise.

He needed to get a call off to his team.

Where could he ditch the bike? He'd hotwire a car if need be. Thank Christ he and Julius had spent hours as kids testing their skill on an old beat-up Chevy their dad owned. The knowledge would come in handy today.

They were outside of Spring Valley. That damn needle on the gas gauge didn't tell him how many miles he had left on the tank. He estimated seven, maybe ten at most. Where would that put them on the map?

His mind shot ahead to the next town—which happened to be the home of the Sentry team. They were a good thirteen miles from East Canon, though. But on the outskirts, there would be somewhere to stop and hide the bike. He could make a call and have someone pick them up in minutes.

As he hammered down on the gas, Wren latched on to him even tighter. She had to be terrified. He would never, ever admit to being afraid...but he could lose her.

He and his brothers had failed one mission before and a young woman died on their watch. The event broke all five of them. It made Judd, Jaren and Jace more determined to succeed in the bodyguard business, while he and Julius shied away from it for a few years.

Only when they got sick of manual labor or spending hours under vehicles in their dad's shop changing oil did they accept Lexis's offer to join Sentry.

I can't lose Wren. I love her.

He was going to get a ring on her finger and send her back to med school. She was too good to let that talent slip away. Then...he'd put a child inside her. Start his own little Abel brood.

As soon as he hit the outskirts of East Canon, an idea hit. Maybe the craziest fucking idea he'd ever had.

The church where it all started.

He could hide his bike in the gardener's shed behind the building. Darkness had fallen, and that was an advantage. He just needed to get off this bike before it ran out of gas and make that call to his team.

When he geared down, Wren squeezed him so hard that he had to draw harder to pull air into his lungs. He felt like stroking his Harley and telling her what a good girl she was for making it so far on little gas and making promises to take better care of her next time.

Cutting the headlight, he rolled into the empty parking lot and toward the shed. As soon as he saw the padlock, he inwardly cussed. Picking it was easy but would take up precious seconds.

He stopped and lowered the kickstand. "Get off. Hurry!"

* * * * *

Jennings's urgent whisper had Wren leaping off the motorcycle as if it was molten-hot steel. He jumped off too and ran up to the shed, fishing in his pocket as he closed the distance. "Wren, get over here."

She did his bidding.

"Place your back to the shed. Try to blend in. We can't be seen."

A shudder racked her. Nausea fisted her gut, making it cramp.

She threw herself against the shed wall and flattened her back and arms to it. "What's going on?"

"The bike's out of gas. We have to hide it."

"In here?"

"Yes. I'm picking the…" He broke off in silence for several thunderous beats. Then she heard the soft metallic click of him forcing the lock. "Yes! Stay right there. I'll push the bike inside."

Feeling helpless wasn't new to Wren. Being a target was. Her breaths came in short bursting pants as she watched for hidden dangers and Jennings pushed the bike inside the shed. He locked it again and yanked out his phone.

Just then, a set of headlights cut through the darkness and panned far too close to the shed. She let out a cry that cut off as Jennings locked a hand on her arm and forced her into a dead run.

They slammed into the wall of the church. The lights turned the corner.

"Goddammit. What are the chances that they're coming here on a Thursday night? They're not on schedule until tomorrow." He moved down the wall, towing her behind him. They reached the back door. He tried the handle — and it opened.

The lights washed over the building right where they'd been standing before Jennings thrust her through the door.

The nightmare was back in full force complete with the smell and the dingy beige walls of the back room where Viper had brought her.

Jennings tried another door, found it unlocked too, and they slipped into the dark room.

Her heart beat so loud that she couldn't hear a thing. She saw his lips moving and knew he was speaking to someone on the phone but didn't make out a word.

Suddenly, his head snapped up, his gaze directed at the closed door.

"Fucking hell!" He latched on to her wrist and towed her across the room. "We have to hide."

"Where?"

His eyesight in the dark was far superior to hers. She hadn't even seen the coffin until he cracked it open.

"In here."

She shook her head. "No way!"

Footsteps sounded. The door cracked open.

Jennings threw himself into the coffin, dragging her in behind him. She landed on his hard body, knocking the air out of her lungs. What did it matter if she couldn't breathe? They were going to die anyway.

Then Jennings snaked out an arm and lowered the lid on top of them, sealing their fate.

Chapter Seventeen

Darkness swallowed them. The harsh rasp of Wren's breaths filled the space. He had to calm her down.

His idea to jump inside the coffin might be up there on the list with killing Viper. His team would never let him live that down either. His brothers would bring it up every time they got together and bust him about it.

If the guys who entered the room planned to load the coffin with drugs, he and Wren were fucked.

His weapon lay along his spine, out of reach.

First on the list — soothe Wren. It probably wasn't the right time to tell her about Lark getting locked in one of these coffins.

His arm was locked behind her. There was little space in this thing, but he managed to shift his arm into a more comfortable position to hold her. He also brushed his lips over her temple.

"It's okay, baby," he murmured in the lowest voice possible.

She shivered but didn't respond. Long seconds passed where neither spoke. Beyond the walls of their tomb he heard shuffling noises, and then voices.

"Take everything here to the sanctuary. Boss's orders."

Sanctuary. In his mind's eye, Jennings saw the mausoleum where they'd loaded drugs into the drawers.

"Every single thing? Are you sure?"

"Yeah. Nothing left behind."

"We've never done that before. We only move things in small runs."

"I know. But this is what we were told to do, so shut your gob and get to work."

Jennings's mind raced. They were sitting ducks here. His impulse to hide Wren was a bad one, but fighting his way out of the situation came with more risks. Now they were screwed. Without his gun, they were dead.

With his lips at Wren's temple, he murmured, "Reach underneath me and get my gun."

She gave a small, swift shake her of head, the movement miniscule in the tight space. "I can't."

"You can. I need you to place it in my hand."

Her chest heaved against his. Her body vibrated with tension. The shuffle of items being shifted around outside the coffin had her tensing even more.

"Baby..."

The heavy thump of an object hit the lid. She jerked hard and in the same move delved her hand underneath him. She yanked the weapon free and felt

214

around for his hand until he closed his fingers on the grip.

All that wiggling—and having the woman he lusted after with every fiber of his being on top of him—had him achingly hard and brought a groan to the edge of his lips.

She froze. *"Now?"*

His cock swelled against her. "You know how much I want you," he whispered back.

"But now?"

Okay, so it wasn't great timing to get a boner for his woman when they were stuck in a coffin together. This might be somebody else's kink, but he could think of far better ways to fuck Wren.

Two more thumps on the lid of the coffin made her jump again. He tightened his hold on the weapon, prepared to act the instant that lid cracked open.

But another box hit the top—good news. If they were stacking crap on top of the coffin, then they didn't plan on opening it to fill it with drugs.

A low noise of a phone ringing brought a soft gasp to Wren's lips. Jennings strained to hear the one-sided conversation.

"You're kidding. Okay, you're not kidding. But you're sure you really want to do this? There must be half a million dollars' worth of drugs here."

Silence was as loud as thunderclaps while the speaker listened. Then he let out a sigh, barely audible through the thick lid and fabric lining.

"Okay, if you're sure. Boss's orders."

"What was that about?" asked the second guy in the room.

"Boss wants us to burn it all down."

If Wren's cry was any louder they'd be discovered. Jennings held her tighter.

"No evidence," the guy said.

"So what do we do? Just build a fire on top of the coffin?"

His chest blazed. How was he going to get them out of this?

"Light the church candles in that corner. Tip one over."

* * * * *

The sound of a heavy metal object hitting the floor penetrated all the way through the coffin walls. Wren pictured the whole thing—two stupid thugs piling drugs on top of the coffin, lighting the candlesticks in the corner, then knocking one to the floor.

None of that mattered now. She and Jennings had to get out of here before the coffin went up in flames.

For a beat, Jennings was totally silent.

She could almost hear the cogs of his brain turning. She just hoped they weren't grinding to a halt.

"What are we going to do?" Her voice hovered on the edge of panic, which only made her terror intensify.

"Can you move to the side at all? I need my legs to kick the lid open."

She wiggled around but couldn't move more than a hair. "I can't!"

"Slide your leg as far as you can to your right."

Ordering her own body to move in a certain way wasn't usually a thought in her head. *This* brand of concentration made her break out in a sweat. Her head hurt too.

Oh wait—that was the toxic fumes seeping through the crack in the coffin.

Jennings edged his knee up. "Can you move a little more?"

"There's no room!"

"I know, love. Try to be calm."

She forced her leg to the side, giving him enough room to bend his knee all the way. She couldn't see a thing in here.

"Oh god." Her voice quavered and she felt ill.

"Why do you sound like you're about to freak out?"

"Because I am! I just realized how much I hate confined spaces."

"Don't think about it. Pretend you're on top of me and we're just having fun locked in a closet together."

"That's your idea of *fun*? Being locked in a *closet*?"

He huffed out a noise that might be a laugh or a grunt. If it was the former, she would most *definitely* make him pay for laughing at a time like this—right after they got out of here.

"Can you hurry? I'd rather not burn to death in a coffin piled high with a bunch of drugs in the back room of a church!"

He shifted around. His abs rolled underneath her. His thighs bulged against hers...*so* close to her pussy.

Oh no. Her libido ramped into overdrive. All of a sudden, she understood how he got hard when she wiggled.

Admitting that she was in the same state of arousal went against the grain.

On the other hand...it could offer some very good incentive.

"Jennings?"

"Yeah, love."

"I'm getting turned on by your body moving against mine."

He stilled.

"I really want you."

"That's the adrenaline talking. But hold on to it. I'm gonna—" His muscles locked as he attempted to kick open the lid. A sharp bead of light knifed into her eyes when the lid cracked an inch before slamming shut again.

Acrid smoke seeped into the tight space.

"Great! Now we're sharing a small amount of oxygen *and* sucking in noxious fumes!"

"You'll lose your voice from the orgasms I give you when this is all over faster than the fumes will take it out."

The next time he shoved the lid with his boot, the crack of light appeared brighter. Something struck the floor.

Excitement made her nerves vibrate. "A box fell off! Do that again!"

He kicked at the lid again and again. Several more things toppled off.

His voice came out gritty. "When I get this lid up next time, you roll onto your hip. You're going to bear the weight for a few seconds, but you're a badass—you can handle it. It will give me enough space to get the leverage I need. Ready?"

"Yes!"

He kicked upward. The lid cracked, and she jammed herself onto her side. The weight of the lid and whatever rested on top, trapping them inside, crushed her shoulder and thigh.

Smoke billowed in, black and oily.

"Help me push!"

Using all her strength, she put her shoulder into the action. Boxes hit the floor. The noise of flames devouring everything in their path roared in her ears.

Jennings got his arm up. In one enormous shove, he forced the lid open. He leaped out of the coffin and dragged her out behind him. Her legs wobbled, her knees like water when she saw flames licking the corner where the blaze started. Paint bubbled and melted off the wall. The ceiling was engulfed.

An explosion came from the door. They both whirled as men rushed in.

Jennings swept out an arm and threw her behind him.

His bulky shoulder obstructed her view. Then she heard Julius.

"Jesus Christ, bro. Get out — now!"

He latched on to her hand and whirled her in front of him. "Take her!"

"Livingston, go!" Julius ordered the other man who'd burst in.

Hands closed on her shoulders. She didn't have time to glance back to see why Jennings wasn't getting her to safety himself.

When fresh, cold air absent of toxic fumes hit her face, she filled her lungs with gulp after gulp. Then she realized the rest of her senses were going haywire. She blinked rapidly to clear her vision.

She couldn't be staring at two men rather than three. She swung her head, searching for the man she needed just as much as the precious air filling her lungs.

Then she had her answer.

Julius bolted back inside after Jennings.

Chapter Eighteen

Wren was safe. Nothing else mattered.

Jennings held up his phone and panned it over the drugs and destruction, video recording it all before the evidence was destroyed.

He twisted from the wall of heat. Wren. He had to get to Wren. He wouldn't be okay until she was in his—

Pain blasted through his skull. A roar hit his lips. Fury back-built like the fire that surrounded him.

Good—he needed that. He clung to it like a lifeline because he refused to pass out.

Weapon raised, he whirled and faced one of the thugs who slipped back in. Judging by the duffel bag he gripped, he'd come to rescue as many bags of drugs as possible.

At such close range, Jennings didn't need to aim. He squeezed the trigger. The sound was almost lost under the roar of flames.

The man fell with a scream.

Another guy rushed in out of nowhere. Holding steady, Jennings prepared to take the kill shot.

Then he saw who it was and let his weapon swing to his side. "Julius!"

His brother stared at the man writhing on the floor. "Look at you, always making shit harder. Couldn't you have just killed him? Now I have to drag him out of the burning church and save his useless ass."

Despite the pain radiating through his skull, he laughed. "You carry him. I've got your six."

With a sigh, Julius hooked the fallen criminal under the arms. His body hit Julius's shoulder. Julius's ranting was loud enough to be heard over the fire. "Days ago it was a guy in your trunk. Now this. No idea why Mom made me the big brother. You could be cleaning up my messes."

His brothers irritated the hell out of Jennings, but he ignored him as he led the way out of the building with Julius right behind.

Smoke clogged all the corridors, cloaking the exits. He held his breath and ran for it, checking over his shoulder every few steps to make sure Julius was following.

Through the thick gray smoke, he spotted the door. Using his shoulder, he slammed through it and staggered outside. Wildly, he scanned the parking lot.

Wren. Where was she?

His stare landed on a pair of people. Livingston and Wren seemed to be in a tug of war. He grasped her arm, holding her back, and she strained with all her might to get away.

"Let me go! I have to get him!"

"Julius has him! Don't you hear that hissing? The gas is turned on. The place is about to blow!"

Jennings raced away from the building, right toward Wren.

The relief washing over her beautiful face left him ready to find a jeweler on his way out of town and buy a ring immediately.

"Go!" His vocal cords threatened to sever from the force of his bellow. He jerked his arm back and forth to wave her forward.

This all happened in a blink. He twisted back to help Julius get the criminal to safety before the explosion took them all out.

An SUV was parked feet away with all the doors open. Livingston practically threw Wren inside. When he slammed the door, she turned her face to the glass, watching him pound his way across the short span of pavement.

He and Julius hurled the criminal into the back seat and leaped in behind him.

"Drive!" His order set Livingston in motion. He gassed the vehicle.

"Oh...my...god." Wren's words came at the same time the church exploded.

The vehicle rocked from the blast. Livingston stomped the gas harder and sped away from the scene.

Wren twisted in the passenger seat to look at him, her eyes wide and round. "Jennings, your bike!"

"Don't worry about it now. We're out. You're safe." He locked gazes with her.

Her bottom lip trembled. The love in her eyes burned as bright as the intense flames.

When they hit the road leading to East Canon, he realized the man he'd shot was stirring. He glared down at him.

The guy cracked an eye.

"You damn near killed us!" Jennings cocked his fist and slammed it into his face.

The guy passed out again.

"Damn, Jennings. Remind me never to fuck with you." Livingston's dry tone brought an unexpected giggle from Wren.

She pressed her fingers to her lips to hold it in.

That sound was the water of life. It was the very air that Jennings breathed.

He reached over the front seat to touch her shoulder. When her soft fingers rested over his, he let his eyes slip closed on the pure love coursing through his body.

He'd get her out of this place. Give her the chance to rest and heal. Then he'd do everything in his power to make her the happiest woman alive. If she wanted that medical degree, he'd help her get it. If she wanted her brother transferred to a bigger, better facility far away from here, he had the connections to make that happen.

He brushed his thumb over her delicate finger. One day — soon — he'd put a ring on it.

"What now?" Livingston's question brought him back to the present.

Turning his head, he locked gazes with Julius. "Get this motherfucker to the cops. Or a hospital. We drop Wren with the other women. I have to get on that plane for El Paso. Problem is, I missed the food drop-off and ran out of the bar. The Disciples will know something's wrong."

Julius eyed him. "What's the plan?"

"I make excuses. Say I realized the woman was an imposter and I took care of her."

Wren gave a small squeak.

He sent her a soft look of apology.

Julius grabbed his phone and brought it to his ear. "Lexis. We're dropping a criminal at the hospital. He's bleeding but not in danger of dying — yet. Yeah, get the cops to meet us. Where are the women right now?"

He listened for a moment and then ended the call in a few short words and grunts.

When he put the phone away, he nudged the unconscious man. "He's taking up most of the seat."

"Why do you think I put the last guy in the trunk?"

Wren whipped around. "What? You put a man in the trunk, Jennings?"

Livingston gulped back a laugh.

Wren's gaze fixed on Jennings. "Who did you put in the trunk?"

"It's not important. I'm doing my job."

Her face crumpled. "You can't get on that plane. It's dangerous. When we were in the bar, those guys recognized me. They know you killed the drug dealer."

He shrugged. "I'll say it was a crime of passion. I wanted you — I took you. Simple as that."

She shuddered. "Even if they buy that story, you're going to be with the vice president of the Disciples. They don't mess around, Jennings. If they find out who you are, they'll kill you."

"I've known that since I started this op. To stay in my role, I have to get on that plane. Trust me, baby. I know what I'm doing. There's no way out of this now."

He wanted to tell her how much he loved her. That his feelings were bone-deep. But now wasn't the time for sweet confessions. He'd save that for when she was naked in his arms.

He reached out and stroked a fingertip down to the point of her delicate chin. "You'll be safe in lockdown with the rest of the Sentry wives."

She opened her mouth to protest, but whatever she read on his face made her jaws snap shut. She twisted forward again.

* * * * *

"Abel, you're live. We got you on the map."

Jennings didn't respond to Lexis's statement. Any outward acknowledgement would be a red flag to Cole. He'd managed to blend in for this long. He was confident that he could keep flying under the radar.

He'd lost the listening device in the church when it blew up. But the communication device in his ear was equally small and would go unnoticed. And when he climbed into the van with Cole, Jennings didn't pick up on any tension.

They didn't head to the main terminal of the airport. Instead, they circled to another gate where they accepted shipments. A cargo plane sat at the ready.

Giving no indication that this was odd, Jennings followed Cole's lead and moved from the van to the tarmac. Cole climbed a set of metal folding stairs into the aircraft. As Jennings trailed behind, he ducked his head under the doorframe.

As soon as he entered the plane, he noted the motorcycles. Twenty in total, without their tires, all strapped to the plane walls to hold them in place.

Cole was staring at him.

Jennings let out a low whistle. "Good inventory here, boss man."

He nodded. "You know it." When the man walked with a swagger to a seat along one wall, Jennings did the same.

"Sit down. I want to talk to you before we take off."

As if he had no sins blemishing his reputation, he sank to the chair and directed his attention to Cole. "What's up?"

His direct gaze held the same dark gleam it usually did. But Jennings read something else in his eyes.

"We know you killed Viper."

Jennings bobbed his head as though deep in thought. "Knew it wouldn't take long for you to find out."

"You killed our man."

"He had the girl. You saw her. She's worth it."

He cocked a brow at Jennings expectantly.

"Viper wasn't managing his territory right anyway. He murdered a guy and left a witness alive. I wanted the girl. I knew I could handle shit better than Viper did. End of story."

"End of story…"

"Yeah, man. You would do the same. Don't tell me you wouldn't."

He snorted. "True."

"So we good?"

Cole's brow hiked up again. "I don't know. Are we?"

"Sure, man." He extended a fist for Cole to bump his knuckles against. "Now, what's with the bikes? Do we get to sample the goods when we land?"

"No. They're being sold."

"Too bad. Not often a man gets to see this many quality bikes in one spot." He glanced at his surroundings, taking in every inch of the plane's interior. He noted the exits as well as the location of the cockpit. "This craft belong to the club?"

"Nah, man. It's rented."

"Gotcha."

Just then the pilot came on the intercom, telling them to fasten their seatbelts. Jennings huffed out a laugh as he clipped the seatbelt around his waist.

"Don't suppose we get booze on this flight."

Cole laughed. "Not unless you brought a bottle."

"I would have if I'd known."

The engine had been a low whir, making it easy to talk, but now it geared up to a loud roar. Getting in the air took no time, and when the aircraft leveled at cruising altitude, Jennings kicked out one leg, settling in.

The Disciples weren't in the bike trade. Not even illegal parts moved through the club. So why were they transporting so many?

His mind drifted to the end game, but since he didn't know what that was, he couldn't plan for it. So many times during this op, he'd flown by the seat of his pants, and he didn't mind doing it again.

Only now, he had a woman relying on him. She hadn't told him that she had feelings for him. He could be deluding himself that she cared. But there was no way to fake that expression on her beautiful face when he was moving inside her.

Cole unhooked his seatbelt and got to his feet.

Jennings looked up at him. "Feel free to move around the cabin?"

His joke fell on deaf ears. Cole swung around and waved a hand.

Jennings's chest tightened when a Disciple stepped out from around some crates.

"Bring out the girl."

Jennings whipped off his belt and leaped to his feet as the biker shoved Wren in front of him.

Oh god. They'd taken her. Sentry hadn't kept her safe. His bowels ran cold as he met her terrified stare.

Chapter Nineteen

Jennings's shoulders flexed. Wren realized he'd reached behind his spine and whipped out a gun.

"Let her go. Now." His tone was loud, controlled. But the tight set of his jaw told her that he was far from calm.

"We brought her along as insurance, Jay. Or is it Abel?"

Cole's words hit her like boulders. Each one barreled into her stomach, threatening to fold her in half. The plane rocked underfoot, and she braced her feet to stay upright.

The man who'd ripped her out of the house where she'd been told to stay with the other women grabbed her by the arm, fingers biting into her flesh. She stifled a scream.

No way would she give this asshole the satisfaction of hearing her terror anymore. When he'd dragged her out of the house with a hand locked over her mouth, she *couldn't* scream.

Then he threw her in the back of a van. That shriek had been bloodcurdling, but he quickly silenced her with a backhand across the cheek.

When he loaded her into the cargo plane, he threatened to gut Jennings in front of her if she made so much as a squeak, so she'd remained silent ever since.

Her breaths came in ragged puffs, and it didn't have anything to do with the altitude.

"Let her go." He forced the words through his firm lips.

"Not a chance. You deceived us. For *months*. Now you're going to pay for it." Cole's eyes glittered with so much malice that Wren's heart started to pound faster.

Jennings gripped his weapon more firmly. "Let her go. It's me you want."

Did he see the imperceptible nod that the thug who'd kidnapped her gave the other biker?

All of a sudden, Jennings jerked around as a bullet pinged off the wall of the plane. There was no holding back the scream constricted in her throat then. It ricocheted along with several more gunshots.

A huge arm knocked her off her feet, sending her flying backward into the row of bikes. Pain blasted through her hip and outer thigh.

She rolled onto her hands and knees, scrabbling on the floor to push herself upright. As she glanced up, she saw Jennings dart to the side. A bullet whizzed past him, and he ducked out of the way.

"No!" The yelp tore from her lips.

233

Bullets flew around the metal cage they were all trapped in. If Jennings was struck...her heart would be ripped out.

She loved that man with every throb of her heart. She couldn't lose him.

A bullet slammed into the bike beside her. Metal sheared open, revealing bags of heroin.

She had to help Jennings. She couldn't just stand here doing nothing.

Steely fingers dug into her ribs, and the biker dragged her forward. A gun barrel dug into her temple.

But the pain reflected in Jenning's eyes cut through her more than fear for her own life.

"Don't hurt her." He collapsed to his knees. His weight thumped hard on the floor of the plane.

She stared at him. Her hot whisper was raspy. "Don't do this!"

"It's me you want," he grated out. "She didn't do anything wrong. She saved Matthews."

Cole looked between her and Jennings. Then he nodded for the biker to let her go. When he released her, she pitched forward onto her hands and knees. The guy poked his gun at Jennings's chest.

No. No, no, no. She had to do something. Had to help the man she loved.

"You're not going to get away with what you've done, Abel. You want justice, this is it." Then Cole moved in on Jennings.

Heart hammering, Wren threw a wild look around. Then she saw the cargo net hanging from hooks on the wall, unused. Daring a quick glance to see if the Disciples were watching, she saw they weren't and reached for the net.

In a few quick moves, she unhooked it. Jennings didn't look her way, and for that she was grateful. If he gave away what she was doing, they'd kill her. Then she couldn't save him.

The vice president fixed the gun barrel on Jennings's head. "Ready to meet your maker?"

She didn't give Jennings a chance to answer. She hurled the net over the man and leaped on his back. Her weight wasn't enough to take him to the ground, but she wrapped her arm around his neck with all her strength.

* * * * *

Cole fell to his knees and threw Wren to the floor. Her fragile body bowed with the impact. She rolled, head lolling to the side.

A roar exploded from Jennings's throat. In one maneuver, he leaped to his feet and threw all of his body weight at the man attacking his woman.

She was still fighting like a wild animal. The vicious kick she aimed at his jaw sent Cole's head snapping backward. Blood poured out of his mouth.

Jennings snatched up his weapon and pumped a bullet into the other biker. Then he stomped on Cole's neck, pinning him to the floor.

"Don't fucking move," he ground through his teeth. "I want you alive so you can sit and rot in a jail cell. But if you so much as blink, I will pull this trigger."

Cole glared up at him. "Go ahead and shoot me."

"Wren?"

"Y-yes?"

"Grab me one of those ratchet straps holding the bikes together. Bring it to me."

He kept his gaze trained on his adversary but heard her whimper.

"Calm down, honey. Take your time unhooking the strap."

When she worked the fastener open, the bike hit the floor with a crash. Bags of drugs spilled out of the gas tank.

He held out a hand and Wren placed the strap in it. "Can you hold the gun on him?" he asked her.

"I'd rather not!"

"Then you wrap that strap around him." He jammed his boot into Cole's neck until his eyes bulged. "Move and I'll shoot you."

He continued to glare at Jennings while Wren did as instructed.

"Slide that end through the fastener. That's it, baby. You're doing great. Now tighten it down."

The noise of the ratchet being tightened mixed with the hum of the plane engine. The floor had spatters of blood that he prayed she didn't notice. He didn't want her freaking out at this altitude.

She gave the strap one last crank and then released a sigh. "That's the tightest it goes."

"Good, love." He held out his arm. "Come here."

Her eyes blazed with tears and emotion. Stumbling over to him, she let out a cry and threw herself into his hold. He clasped her tightly to his side and held her trembling body for a long moment.

After she recovered a bit, he gave her a gentle nudge toward the seat. "Go sit down. I'm going to make sure this fucker is taken care of."

Wren moved to the seat, and Jennings grabbed hold of Cole and dragged him to the wall of the plane. There, he fastened him to some hooks and left him.

When he returned to Wren, she popped to her feet and flung her arms around him. "Oh my god. Jennings, I was so afraid. I thought I'd lose you. I l-love…l-love you!"

Her confession bored into his brain, seeped to his bones and filled the hollow cavern in his chest. She nestled her body against him, and his heart overflowed with even more emotion.

Hooking his finger under her chin, he lifted her face up to his. Holding her gaze, he leaned in slowly and pressed his lips to hers. She melted into the caress, one hand looped around his nape.

"I love you so damn much, baby." He crushed her to him and buried his nose in her hair, breathing her scent.

"When they burst into the house and took me—"

He jerked his head up. "What about the other women?"

She shook her head, eyes frantic. "I don't know. I don't know what happened to them!"

"I'm going to find out." He reached into his pocket and pulled out his phone.

"Can you make a call?"

"No. But I can text." His thumbs worked fast as he shot a message to Lexis.

They took Wren. She's with me in the air. Subjects subdued. We're safe.

Wren glanced at the dead man and then away.

"He's definitely subdued." She shuddered.

"He got what he had coming to him." He shot off another text.

Where are the women?

Lexis responded immediately. *Safe. But Livingston's house is gone.*

238

He looked up from his screen into Wren's eyes. "What does he mean by 'gone?'" she whispered.

As if he heard her question, Lexis replied: *They burned it down.*

Chapter Twenty

Jennings climbed from behind the wheel of the rental car. After so many hours on the road from El Paso, his cramped legs had begun to feel like he'd never straighten them. But after they landed and the authorities hauled away the Disciples and confiscated the contents of the cargo plane, Wren flat-out refused to get back in the air.

He didn't mind though. It gave them plenty of time to talk about what happened.

He also had time for a very, very important side trip to take care of personal business...

As he circled the vehicle to the passenger door where Wren sat, he stared at the charred, blackened ruin of Livingston's house.

Fuck. They really had burned it down. Again.

The original home had been a complete loss months ago. Livingston and Dove rebuilt, but they weren't even finished with the interior as far as Jennings knew. Now this...

Wren saw the house and let out a gasp. "Oh nooo. Poor Dove!"

He assisted her to the sidewalk, his arm still around her. "What matters is no one was hurt."

"But they were starting on the baby's nursery. She'll be so devastated at the loss."

"I'm sure they both are."

They stood on the sidewalk staring at the ruin of the new construction. The contractors had just installed the siding.

Wren shook her head. "Your jobs are dangerous. The Disciples still managed to find me in hiding. What if this"—she waved at the burned home—"happens to us?"

Grasping her shoulder, he swung her to face him. Their gazes connected.

"But that pastor—"

"The pastor wasn't coming to the home to track you down, Wren. He was there trying to act like a pastor and throw people off the scent that he's a criminal. The entire Disciples club is wiped out and everyone associated with it is behind bars."

"But there will be more dangerous groups."

"It's why..." He faltered, glancing down.

She caught his gaze again. "Jennings?"

"It's why I've been thinking about taking you back to my hometown. Start fresh."

She shook her head. "You can't do that. Sentry needs you. Your team needs you." She twisted to look up at the house again. The gray clouds scudding across the sky seemed to weigh down the mood even more. But when she turned those eyes on him, his heart lifted on a swirl of love.

"We both have dreams, Jennings. I won't let you walk away from your team."

"And I won't let you live in fear. If that means we leave this place and I work in my dad's garage, then I'm more than willing to."

The noise of car tires on the street made him reluctantly look away from Wren. The SUV rolling toward them was familiar. So was the man at the wheel.

When Livingston parked, all the doors opened. Lexis got out of the front seat. Julius from the back.

The trio approached him and Wren slowly.

Jennings reached out to Livingston first, bringing him in to thump his back. "Damn, bro. I'm sorry about the house."

"So am I. With Dove so close to delivering the baby, it was a blow. But at least she's safe. We can put up a portable crib in the house we're renting."

They drew apart, and he reached for Lexis next.

"Glad to have you home. Good work, Abel."

"Thanks."

"The bar's been shut down. The personnel at the church arrested. The guy Wren saw at the nursing facility — the pastor behind the operation with the Disciples — in custody."

Jennings stepped back. "That's good. Real good."

Finally, Julius stepped forward. Their gazes met. His brother jerked a thumb at Jennings. "The lengths this guy will go to in order to prove me wrong."

Jennings ducked his head to hide the grin stretching across his face. "Are you admitting you were wrong about me being able to pull off this op?"

"That and..." Julius looked at Wren.

He understood what his brother wasn't saying.

"I'll go all the way to the altar to prove you wrong on *that*, Julius."

She sucked in a gasp. Jennings snaked an arm around her waist, pulling her snug against his side. "I mean it, baby. I aim to marry you—as soon as possible."

When he studied her face, her cheeks were pink and her eyes brighter. "We're tired after that drive. Did Livingston say there's a cookout?"

"Yup—my place." Lexis twitched his head, indicating they should all get back in their vehicles and follow him. "Last guy there has to grill the steaks."

The guys quickly jumped into the SUV, but Jennings hung back with Wren.

She rested her palms on his chest, tipping her face up to his. "You're going to get stuck manning the grill."

"I don't mind. I actually enjoy it. But Wren..."

243

She searched his face. "Yes?"

"There's something else I want to talk to you about."

She stilled. "What is it?"

"Sentry wants to offer you a contract."

Her eyelids fluttered. "What? A contract?"

Judging by her expression, he'd caught her off guard. Either that or she was waiting for him to say something else.

"Yeah. The task force won't only consist of four people forever. And we're going to need someone who can provide medical care to us. You know, patch us up when we need it."

She shook her head. "But I don't have a degree."

"Not yet. They've offered to pay for you to finish medical school in return for devoting some of your time to the team."

She gaped at him. "Are you serious? How did you manage that?"

He stepped closer to her, cupping her face. "Your fiancé is a pretty smooth talker when he puts his mind to it."

"My *fiancé!*"

In one smooth move, he dropped to one knee.

The diamond ring he pulled out of his jeans pocket glinted. She let out a loud gasp and pressed her hands over her mouth.

"Jennings!" Her eyes swam with tears.

His heart thumped faster. "Wren. You're the love of my life. I never want to be separated from you. Will you be my wife?"

Her eyes swam with tears that spilled over and ran down both cheeks. When she couldn't find words, she simply bobbed her head. Then she dropped her hands and threw her arms around his neck.

"Yes! Yes, I'll be… Oh my god, you just asked me to marry you! You're not fling material after all! Wait till I tell the girls—"

He cut her off by sliding the ring onto her finger. Then he surged to his feet, hauling her up with him…and claimed her mouth in an endless kiss.

* * * * *

The door blasted open. Jennings didn't even pause in kissing Wren before he whipped her to face the wall.

Her palms flattened against the drywall, her chest heaving from the lust blazing through her body.

"Don't move." His voice burned with its own level of frustration. Who could blame him after he'd fingered her to completion in the car and took nothing for himself?

She heard the lock click. Then his hands landed on her hips. He spread his fingers, spanning her ass.

He dropped his lips to her ear. "You wore this dress just to drive me crazy."

"Yes," she whispered.

"Well, it worked. Now I'm going to show you just how crazy." He whipped the silky dress up, hooked his finger in the string of her thong—soaked after the release he gave her in the car—and tugged it aside.

"I'm going to bury my cock in your pussy, Wren."

Her breath hitched. "Right here?" She'd never done it standing up.

"Yup. The hotel staff is going to know my name by the time I'm finished with you too."

The clinking noise that followed made her fingers curl against the wall. A dark heat coiled low in her stomach as she imagined his long fingers working open his belt and the fly of the suit pants he'd worn to the big dinner thrown in Sentry's honor.

Her nipples puckered in anticipation. Twisting her head to the side, she spotted the intense concentration on his face as he sidled up behind her.

When she felt the string of her thong snap, she let out a low cry. The sound transformed into a primal moan as he nestled his mushroomed cock at her entrance.

"Take me, Jennings!"

"You want my cock?" He pushed an inch inside her.

"Yes!"

"Like this? Ohhh fuck! You're so wet I can't even keep from sliding in!" He sank balls-deep in one swift glide.

He stilled, and she did too. Her gaze ticked up to her ring finger and the engagement ring settled at the base of it, a beautiful reminder of what this night meant to both of them. Their announcement to the Sentry ladies at the dinner had been welcomed and toasted so many times. The guys got tipsy on bourbon and the women, all pregnant, had to keep running to the restroom after sipping so much sparkling water.

Wren arched her back, and Jennings bottomed out inside her. They shared a groan, and then he was churning his hips. Slamming home. Jerking back out and fucking her deep with each stroke.

Her body hummed. Reaching around her, he cupped her breasts and sent her sailing toward the second orgasm that night.

"That's it, baby. I feel you clenching around me. *Pulsing.*"

She whimpered.

"Come on me, baby. Come for me!"

He swished his thumb across her nipple, shooting her body into overdrive. The slap of his hard body against hers, the steel sinking into her pussy over and over, drove her to her tiptoes as her release hit.

"Yessss. Fuck yes!" He pumped into her faster. The tension inside him reached a pinnacle before he let out a low rumble. Hot splashes of cum hit her insides. Her pussy squeezed on the sensation as her own bliss washed through her.

She dropped her forehead to the wall and breathed through the intense aftershocks shaking her apart. Jennings wound his strong arms around her middle and he kissed the side of her neck.

"My beautiful love. I've had the best night of my life with you."

She lifted a hand and lay her palm on his cheek. "So have I. But it's not over…"

He chuckled. "You're right about that. I'm just getting warmed up."

They ended up in the shower with his fingers teasing her clit. She hit her knees to suck him, but that lasted all of a minute before he dragged her out of the bathroom.

They never made it to the bed and he gave her another orgasm on the hotel room carpet.

Finally, he scooped her up and lay her on the bed with all the tenderness a woman could only dream of having from a lover.

Hovering over her, he stared into her eyes. "I love you, Wren. I'm going to make you the happiest woman alive."

Her heart pattered faster for the man she had grown so close to in such a short span of time. She cupped his face. "I love you. You've done so much for me."

He blinked. "I put you in danger."

"You saved me from hell. Who knows what Viper would have done to me."

"I dragged you into things you had no business being involved in." He rolled onto his back and slung his forearm over his eyes.

Wren's heart flexed. Leaning over him, she struggled to find a way to soothe the beast inside her man—the one that was telling him that he'd screwed up and damaged her somehow.

"Jennings, you kept me safe the entire time. You told me to trust you. You knew what you were doing."

"I should have gotten you out of here. When that asshole had his hands on you in the plane—" he broke off, throat working.

She touched his arm. "Is that what this is about?"

He tore his arm off his eyes. The dark depths blazed with fury she was sure he directed at himself. "Yes, goddammit. I fucked up. I thought I was keeping you close so you wouldn't get hurt. Then they took you out of the house and put you on that plane. Fucking bullets were spraying everywhere. You could have been killed!"

"But I wasn't." She leaned in to nuzzle him.

"Dammit. My brothers are right. I make bad decisions. I take the dangerous route every time."

She shook her head, rubbing her nose against his. "Absolutely wrong. You did everything right. You infiltrated a motorcycle club and flew under their radar for months. Tonight the FBI honored Sentry because of you."

249

He dragged in a deep breath and let it out slowly.

"Plus...you got the girl."

He looked at her. The blazing passion in the depths of his eyes urged her forward. She climbed on top of him and kissed him even as she slid over his hard erection.

When they began to move, the heat of love fueled them. The emotions built in her chest and he took the lovemaking even higher by staring deep into her eyes.

She curled her toes and tossed back her head as another orgasm hit. Jennings poured his cum into her again and again until they lay spent in each other's arms.

He trailed his fingertips over her spine. "How much time will it take you to finish med school?"

"I only have to complete my residency."

"And you can do that anywhere, right?"

She met his gaze. "Yes. Why?"

"I was hoping we could stay right here. East Canon isn't much. It's rundown. There are no jobs and people are suffering, but—"

"That's all the more reason for me to stay. I've always wanted to do good in the world. I can serve in a community that needs good healthcare. That excites me. Plus, my brother will be getting out of rehab soon. I want to be here for him when he does. Besides...I kind of fell in love with your Sentry family as well. I want to be here for Lark and Dove and

Avalynn. I want to meet their babies and be the favorite aunt."

He chuckled, drawing her closer into the wreath of his arms. "And when do I get to give you a child too?"

Her jaw dropped. "You want that?"

He nodded. "I came from a bigger family. I want to have one of my own. If you do, that is."

She kissed him with a tender brush of her lips across his. "I do."

"Then we better practice some more." He rolled her into the covers and took control until she was gasping out his name and all the love in the world burned between them.

Epilogue

Jennings missed the wind in his hair and the feel of Wren on the back of his Harley. He missed her arms around him and seeing her in his helmet.

Even better was helping his pregnant wife out of their new car.

With a protective arm around her, he guided her to the sidewalk. A pickup rolled up too fast and too close and parked in front of his vehicle.

Wren gasped. "That guy almost took the mirror off our car!"

He didn't need to glance at who was behind the wheel. "That's just Julius being an asshole."

Julius rolled down the window and shouted at him. "Nice swagger wagon, bro!"

He flipped him the bird at the reference to his dad car and earned a laugh for his effort. Grinning, he directed Wren to the front door of the brand-new home that was finally standing in the spot where two others had sat before it.

Wren stopped at the base of the stone steps and stared up at the two-story traditional home. "Quaide and Dove must be thrilled that their home's finished."

He pressed his palm against her lower back to guide her into the house. "It's a real nice neighborhood to raise their daughter."

Wren bobbed her head in agreement. "It's so quiet here."

Jennings swung his head to look at the property next door. The home was a little old-fashioned and could use some modern updates. But it was solid. As was the place across the street.

"I can't wait to get my hands on that baby." She reached to press the doorbell, but the door opened.

Jennings met Livingston's gaze and then slid his stare to the baby he held on his shoulder. Her blonde curls sported a huge pink bow.

"Glad you could make it to our housewarming. C'mon in." He smiled at Wren, who immediately went for the baby.

"Oh my! Look at how much you've grown in just a week. How is my favorite niece?" She reached for the baby, and Livingston handed over his daughter.

"She just burped, so she shouldn't barf on you."

Wren laughed. "Bea and I don't care about a little spit-up, do we, Bea? Oh my god, those curls." She absently dropped her purse where she stood and took off with the baby.

Jennings shook his head and reached for his wife's purse. "Pregnancy brain. She just drops things wherever she's at. Later, she can't find anything.

Good thing I keep watch and gather everything up and put it where it belongs so she can find it later."

Livingston chuckled. "Dove was a little scattered in the middle of her pregnancy too. You want a beer?"

Before he could respond, Julius and Avalynn walked through the open door. His brother toted a baby carrier with their infant son. Julius Jr. kicked his feet and waved his fists, his face screwed up.

Jennings met his brother's stare. "Looks just like his daddy."

He set the baby carrier on the floor, and Avalynn crouched to remove the child from the harness. "JJ is just as demanding as his father too, aren't you, baby boy?" she baby-talked him.

"You just wait, brother. You think you're just buying a car with all the safety features for your family, but pretty soon you're not sleeping because your six-month-old is teething." Julius stifled a yawn behind his hand.

Avalynn stood with the baby in her arms. "You were great with him last night, honey. Julius was up most of the night walking JJ to settle him so I could sleep."

Jennings's chest welled with emotion. Now he was the family man—and he couldn't wait to take care of his own son that was due in a few months' time. He just knew the baby would have Wren's big blue eyes and he'd fall in love a second time.

Suddenly, Dove walked into the entryway. "Come in, everyone! We've got snacks in the kitchen and dinner will be served in an hour." Her gaze fell on Avalynn, and grins broke over both of their faces.

They embraced and then went off to the kitchen, fussing over the angry, teething baby.

"I think Julius could use that beer." Livingston turned and led the way to the kitchen.

When Jennings stepped into the bright, airy, spacious kitchen, he couldn't help but compare it to the one he'd seen in the house next door. But he was soon distracted by Livingston shoving a beer at him, and Lexis sauntered over, cradling his sleeping son in the crook of one arm.

He looked at Julius. "You look tired, Abel. Not sleeping well?"

Julius grunted and cracked open his beer. "Weren't you in the same situation last week?"

"Yup, but Elijah has two new teeth. See?" He pressed a big finger into the sleeping baby's bottom lip, pulling it down to show off two tiny white nubs.

"Nice." Julius tipped back his beer and took a long swallow.

Across the room, the women were gathered around the table where platters of food were set out. The four of them talked and laughed, passing babies between them. Jennings couldn't tear his eyes off Wren for long, though. She was the brightest star in the sky to him. Glowing brighter than all the rest.

255

Livingston clapped him on the shoulder, gaining his attention. "So? How was the house tour?"

He darted a look at Wren again. "Keep your voice down."

"Wait—she doesn't know you looked at the house next door to buy it?"

"No. I wanted to check it out first. I didn't want her to be disappointed if it was a dump."

"And is it?"

"No. It needs some remodeling, but the inspector who looked at it says it's sound."

Livingston nodded. "Are you planning to make an offer?"

"I'm not sure yet. I don't think it's fair to make a big decision like that without Wren being on board."

"Well, you're in the neighborhood. Ask her what she thinks about it."

He eyed his friend. "I'm still not sure I want to live so close to you. You don't have the greatest track record with keeping your homes standing."

Though two of his homes had burned down now, Livingston only laughed. "Third time's the charm." He waved a hand at the beautiful home he'd built for his family.

At that moment, Wren broke away from the ladies and moved toward Jennings. She searched his eyes. "What are you looking so serious about? Did these guys scare you with fatherhood stories?"

He gave her a solemn nod. "Yes."

She slapped him in the arm. "I know you're joking. Come and get some snacks. Dove made these amazing little rolls…"

He shrugged at the guys and allowed his wife to lead him to the food table. His mind wasn't on snacks, though. It was on that house next door.

Buying a home was always the dream. But Wren might not want to live next to the Livingstons. She was still working on her residency and would already have to put that on pause—again—to have the baby that neither of them had expected to come so soon.

She caught his gaze. "What's going on with you, Jennings?"

He studied her beautiful face. There was no point in pretending that he wasn't distracted as hell.

Linking his hand with hers, he tugged. "Come outside with me."

Shooting him a worried glance, she hesitated before nodding.

When they slipped out of the house, his chest grew tight. For some reason, this felt just as momentous in their relationship as seeing that positive sign on their pregnancy test.

He led her down the steps and across the short span of grass between properties.

"Jennings, aren't we trespassing? These people won't want us walking on their lawn!"

"It's okay, baby. Nobody lives here."

He took her to the cracked sidewalk leading to the front door. "Now, the sidewalk needs replaced."

"Okay? What are we doing out here?"

He stopped and took her by the shoulders, positioning her to look at the house. "I don't like the blue either."

"I don't understand."

"This house is for sale, Wren."

She whipped around to look at him. "What are you saying?"

"I looked at the property yesterday."

Her jaw dropped.

"I only wanted to check it out in case it was a good option for us. For our family." He covered her growing belly with his palm. Beneath the skin, their child moved against his hand, filling him with emotion.

"Oh, Jennings…"

"You don't have to agree. I just wanted to put it out there because you know I'm preoccupied with something, and this is weighing on my mind."

She twisted back to look at the house. Without a word, she walked right up on the porch and peered in the tall window flanking the door.

The future slammed him in a rush of images. Wren sitting on a porch swing, their children surrounding her and in her lap. Love in her eyes when she glanced up at him…

She whirled from the window, and her expression wore that same burning love that he envisioned. "When can we look at it together? Today?"

A laugh burst past his lips. He shouldn't be surprised at her excitement, but it warmed him so much.

He moved forward to take her in his arms. She curled against him, and he tucked her close. "I'll call the owner tomorrow and set up a time. But baby, are you sure? We'd be neighbors to the Livingstons."

"I love them both so much! They're like family to us."

He brushed his lips over her brow. "Maybe you don't want to stay in East Canon after you get your degree."

She cupped his jaw. "Silly man. Home is where you are. I love this place. I love your team and their families. I love that you're thinking about our future, Jennings."

He gently pinched her chin and drew her lips up to his. "I love *you*."

She wrapped her arms tighter around him. He may not have her on the back of his bike, but he had her forever.

The tender kiss they shared quickly turned hotter. She rubbed against him, and he grabbed her ass, hitching her tighter against his growing erection.

"Mmm. Maybe we should try out that porch railing. Or maybe the side of the house?"

259

She issued a laugh, but it was throaty enough to tell him that she was affected by their closeness too. "I think that will have to wait until after the housewarming party."

"Speaking of that...we should get back to Livingston's."

Wren pressed her lips against his again. "I love you, Jennings. Thank you for making me a happy woman."

He nuzzled her. "You're my life now. You and our son." He palmed her belly.

"He still needs a name."

"I was thinking Otto."

She shook her head. "Here we go again with your name suggestions."

He grinned. It had become a running joke between them where he threw out names and she shot them all down.

"Boris."

She bit down on her lower lip. "I don't think so."

"Cletus."

She giggled. "Little Cletus Abel will have a hard life."

He grunted. "We've got a lot of decisions to make."

"We're really good at making decisions together. I have no doubt that we'll know the perfect name when we see it. And we'll know if this is our house when we walk through that door together."

They both turned their heads to look at the door. He didn't speak up, but he already knew that this was the place where they'd raise their children and grow old together.

"Hey, Abel! If you're done making out, come back to the party!" Livingston's shout carried across the yards.

He groaned. "Do we really want to live next to that?"

Laughing, she gripped Jennings's hand. "I'm starving, so we're definitely going back to the party."

When they entered the house and he saw all the faces of the people who supported him on every step he took in his journey of life, Jennings knew that he was really home...with Sentry.

READ ON FOR A SNEAK PEEK OF
SHATTERED TIES
SEAL TEAM BLACKOUT
BOOK 1

The cemetery was packed. Before him extended a sea of black among tombstones and limestone angels.

When Rob Bishop became a Navy SEAL, he knew he'd watch good men die.

He just didn't expect it to happen to his buddy, and so soon.

Within the shield of trees surrounding the cemetery, he didn't have to act a certain way. Keep that stiff upper lip. If he wanted, he could rage and let the tears fall in a way most of the SEALs clustered around Whitlock's casket couldn't.

Except Bishop was dry-eyed. His mouth grim. Stiff upper lip in place.

From this distance, he couldn't make out all the words the preacher said, but he'd been to enough funerals for his fallen teammates to know the words by heart. Sunlight glittered in and out of the trees as they fanned in the California breeze. Bishop squinted unblinkingly at the coffin containing his best friend, the guy who always had his six.

Well, Bishop didn't have his, did he? He'd been too late to stop that mercenary from sneaking up on Whitlock and slicing his throat.

Bishop closed his eyes against the image that had been playing on repeat since the event. Awake, asleep, eyes closed or open, it fucking hurt. And he couldn't unsee it.

When he opened his eyes, the coffin was gone — already lowered into the ground. He'd missed it.

"Goodbye, Lock 'n Load." The nickname stuck in his throat. "Godspeed."

He rubbed a hand over his face, the rasp of his heavy beard growth mingling with the whisper of the wind through the trees. Was it his imagination that the notes created by branches and breeze became words?

Take care, Bishop. Never lose your way.

Except he *had* lost his way. He'd left SEAL Team 1 behind. Through deserts and jungles, he lived, breathed and laid down his life for his duty. Now, instead of his dress uniform, he wore a T-shirt, faded jeans and work boots. He'd only ventured into civilization twice since holing up in his remote cabin, and Whitlock's funeral was one.

He needed time to regroup and figure shit out. Watching your best friend fall took its toll on a man.

The lump was back in his throat as a thin wail of mourning reached him. It had to be Whitlock's mother. Bishop should go to her, give his condolences, but he was a damn coward and clung to the shadows of the trees.

One by one, people stepped up to the headstone. Many reached out to touch it in farewell. Only one man remained, and after he paid his respects to the dead, he turned and looked straight at Bishop.

Of course the former SEAL knew he was there. As Sparrow crossed the grassy cemetery in long strides, Bishop stepped out to meet him.

Sparrow saluted him.

"Asshole," Bishop scoffed.

Being part of a special reconnaissance team out here meant jack shit, but seeing Sparrow brought it all back to Bishop — the guts, drive and balls-to-the-wall determination it took to keep the world safe.

Sparrow clamped his hand on Bishop's shoulder and squeezed. "You'll always be one of us, man."

"No, I won't."

"You can't live in the past. Lock 'n Load would want you to move on."

Bishop's chest burned, but he met Sparrow's steady gaze. "I've made my choice."

"Minds can be changed. Take some time for yourself. Regroup. Then join us in SEAL Team Blackout."

Sparrow had been bugging him ever since the day he caught wind of Bishop's resignation to join them. Only Blackout wasn't just any special forces team. They were underground. The most undercover and elite unit.

In order to keep their families and loved ones safe from the dangers they battled every day, they became ghosts. To the outside world, they didn't exist anymore. Joining SEAL Team Blackout meant being handed your own death certificate and the login to a foreign bank account to collect your earnings.

Bishop gave a shake of his head. "Thanks, man, but I'm good where I'm at."

Sparrow eyed him as if his appearance reflected his state of mind. Hell, it might, but what did Bishop care? He just wanted to pay his respects to his friend, jump back in his truck and head to the solitude of his cabin.

Bishop extended a fist. Sparrow looked down at it and then bumped knuckles with him.

They exchanged a chin lift in lieu of goodbye, and Sparrow strode across the cemetery to the parking lot. After a while, Bishop crossed the lawn to the headstone.

The pristine white marble bore Whitlock's name, nickname and dates of birth and death. The sight of the coins placed along the ledge of the stone closed off Bishop's throat again.

He fished in his pocket and ran his thumbnail along the ridges of a coin.

Leaving a penny on the grave of a man who served his country meant the person visited. A nickel meant he and the deceased served at boot camp together. A dime implied the two served in some capacity.

There weren't any quarters there until Bishop pulled one out of his pocket and set it heads up on the ledge.

A quarter meant he'd been there when Whitlock was killed. He'd watched him draw his last breath.

Memories bombarded him like flashes of light from an air raid. He squeezed his eyes shut, digging his hands deep into his pockets. Long moments of silence ticked by.

I'm doing this. I'm moving on.

265

He opened his eyes. A bruised cloud passed in front of the sun, casting him in the shadow shed by Whitlock's headstone.

He issued a grunt that might have once been a chuckle. "If you think you can bully me from the grave into joining up again, you're wrong, Lock 'n Load." He gave the stone and his friend's memory one last nod. "See ya 'round."

1-CLICK YOUR COPY OF SHATTERED TIES

Em Petrova

Em Petrova is a USA Today Bestselling Author who was raised by hippies in the wilds of Pennsylvania but told her parents at the age of four she wanted to be a gypsy when she grew up. She has a soft spot for babies, puppies and 90s Grunge music and believes in Bigfoot and aliens. She started writing at the age of twelve and prides herself on making her characters larger than life and her sex scenes hotter than hot.

She burst into the world of publishing in 2010 after having five beautiful bambinos and figuring they were old enough to get their own snacks while she pounds away at the keys. In her not-so-spare time, she is fur-mommy to a Labradoodle named Daisy Hasselhoff.

Find Em Petrova at empetrova.com

Other Titles by Em Petrova

SEAL Team Blackout
SHATTERED TIES Bishop's Story
RUTHLESS PROTECTION Sparrow's Story
MERCILESS SURVIVAL Ramsey's Story
SAVAGE PAWN Gunnison's Story

DIXON
TANK
PATRIOT
DIESEL
BLADE

The Guard
HIS TO SHELTER
HIS TO DEFEND
HIS TO PROTECT

Moon Ranch
TOUGH AND TAMED
SCREWED AND SATISFIED
CHISELED AND CLAIMED

Ranger Ops
AT CLOSE RANGE
WITHIN RANGE
POINT BLANK RANGE
RANGE OF MOTION
TARGET IN RANGE
OUT OF RANGE

Knight Ops Series
ALL KNIGHTER

HEAT OF THE KNIGHT
HOT LOUISIANA KNIGHT
AFTER MIDKNIGHT
KNIGHT SHIFT
ANGEL OF THE KNIGHT
O CHRISTMAS KNIGHT

Wild West Series
SOMETHING ABOUT A LAWMAN
SOMETHING ABOUT A SHERIFF
SOMETHING ABOUT A BOUNTY HUNTER
SOMETHING ABOUT A MOUNTAIN MAN

Operation Cowboy Series
KICKIN' UP DUST
SPURS AND SURRENDER

The Boot Knockers Ranch Series

PUSHIN' BUTTONS
BODY LANGUAGE
REINING MEN
ROPIN' HEARTS
ROPE BURN
COWBOY NOT INCLUDED
CUPID COWBOYS

COWBOY BY CANDLELIGHT
THE BOOT KNOCKER'S BABY
ROPIN' A ROMEO
WINNING WYOMING
BEDROOM RODEO
STUD RANCH
COWBOY BEEFCAKE

Ménage à Trouble Series
WRANGLED UP
UP FOR GRABS
HOOKING UP
ALL WOUND UP
DOUBLED UP novella duet
UP CLOSE
WARMED UP

Another Shot at Love Series
GRIFFIN
BRANT
AXEL

Rope 'n Ride Series
BUCK
RYDER
RIDGE

WEST
LANE
WYNONNA

The Dalton Boys
COWBOY CRAZY Hank's story
COWBOY BARGAIN Cash's story
COWBOY CRUSHIN' Witt's story
COWBOY SECRET Beck's story
COWBOY RUSH Kade's Story
COWBOY MISTLETOE a Christmas novella
COWBOY FLIRTATION Ford's story
COWBOY TEMPTATION Easton's story
COWBOY SURPRISE Justus's story
COWGIRL DREAMER Gracie's story
COWGIRL MIRACLE Jessamine's story
COWGIRL HEART Kezziah's story

Single Titles and Boxes
THE BOOT KNOCKERS RANCH BOX SET
THE DALTON BOYS BOX SET
SINFUL HEARTS
JINGLE BOOTS
A COWBOY FOR CHRISTMAS
FULL RIDE

Firehouse 5 Series
ONE FIERY NIGHT
CONTROLLED BURN
SMOLDERING HEARTS

Hardworking Heroes Novellas

EM PETROVA
USA TODAY BESTSELLING AUTHOR

Printed in the USA
CPSIA information can be obtained
at www.ICGtesting.com
LVHW011751060624
782520LV00009B/295

9 798879 598759